Other books by the Author
No Relief
Work
Too Late
Quite Contrary
14 Stories

MOVIES

SEVENTEEN STORIES BY STEPHEN DIXON

NORTH POINT PRESS · SAN FRANCISCO · 1983

To Anne and Sophia

The following stories in this collection appeared in slightly dif-
ferent form in the following periodicals, to which the author and
the publisher extend their thanks: *The Massachusetts Review*
("Movies"), *The South Carolina Review* ("Layaways," "Not
Charles," "The Shirt"), *The New England Review* ("Small
Bear"), *The Kansas Quarterly* ("The Barbecue," "Cy"), *The Lit-
erary Review* ("My Dear"), *Story Quarterly* ("The Watch"), *The
North American Review* ("Stop," "Darling"), *Quarterly West*
("The Moviemaker"), *The Dekalb Literary Arts Journal* ("The
Hole"), *Boundary 2* ("Joke"), *Pequod* ("The New Job"), and *The
Yale Review* ("The Frame"). "Layaways" also appeared in *O.
Henry Prize Stories*, 1982 (Doubleday and Co.).

TABLE OF CONTENTS

3   *Movies*

17   *Layaways*

30   *Small Bear*

39   *The Barbecue*

47   *Not Charles*

58   *My Dear*

65   *The Watch*

74   *Stop*

79   *The Moviemaker*

88   *Cy*

100 *The Shirt*

113 *The Hole*

127 *Joke*

130 *The Gold Car*

140 *The New Job*

151 *Darling*

164 *The Frame*

MOVIES

MOVIES

He says "Hey, where you going?" and she says "I told you before, the movies." He says "Wait for me" and she says "Can't, or how long you going to be?" "Couple of minutes" and she says "Please make it snappy." "That's what I said, couple of minutes, quick, zip and snappy, I'm already on my way." "I won't delay you any further by talking about it or encouraging you to. But kind of make it even snappier than you're doing, as you know I hate getting to a movie even half a minute late." "What about a quarter minute late?" he says, putting on his shoes, and she sticks her arms through her coat sleeves and says "Ready?" and he's looking at her, untied shoelaces between his fingers and she opens the door and he says "Hey, wait for me, I was only sitting here wondering why you're acting like this, but I'm ready, I'm ready," and he ties his shoes and grabs his coat off the hook just before he shuts the door.

He's locking the door while she's already down one flight of stairs and rounding the second for the first floor. He runs downstairs and catches up with her at the corner where she's waiting for the light to change or the heavy traffic to pass. He says "You don't have to run, do you? What time the show begin?" "Any minute" and he says "We'll make it. It's only a three-minute walk to the Embassy." "It's at the Symphony, what gave you the idea it was the Embassy?" "Because you said yesterday there was a movie there you wanted to see. But if it's the Symphony let's take a cab." "You have the money for one? Because I don't—I was thinking of a bus." "You can think of a bus while we're in the cab where I'll be a sport for a change. I mean, how many times has that happened with us?" "None?" and he says "Don't be a wiseguy," and flags down a cab.

They drive to the theater. The line for the box office runs along Broadway and then down Ninety-fifth Street past the Thalia Theater and halfway to West End Avenue. She says "I bet the line only started forming like this a few minutes ago. I should have hurried you up more. I'm sure there won't be any tickets left, and if there are, the movie will probably begin while we're on line and I was told especially not to miss the beginning of it." "Don't worry," he says, "it's a big theater with I think a balcony and orchestra both. They'll never start the movie till all the ticket holders are inside; they want our money and not our howling or demands for our money back, right?"

The line begins moving. People in front and back of them are talking about what a great movie they heard it is. "One of the best . . . nothing like it in five years . . . ten . . . the directing . . . you won't believe it I heard . . . a new woman director . . . worked under what's-his-name, the famous German one whose name I just forgot, or is he French with a German-sounding name? Now he's calling her his master with just her first full-length movie and most critics consider him one of the two or three greatest in the world . . . and the acting . . . editing . . . photography . . . color . . . even the sound . . . something totally new, but no tricks like wraparound or wallaround or whatever it is sound . . . also not that avant-garde a movie where it's unintelligible or intentionally obscure to make up for all its deficits . . . it's the real thing . . . a work of art . . . a classic . . . has animation and real acting and mime and puppets and footage from old films separate and combined and sometimes all five going at one time . . . will definitely win most of the awards, I understand . . . already won the three major foreign festival awards for best acting, direction and movie . . . even the screenplay . . . supposed to be truly original . . . better than any fiction book when read . . . going to be published as a book and is being fought over now by the two big book clubs . . . and the costumes . . . makeup . . . incredible things they did with subtitles streaming out of the actors' mouths in a dozen languages and in several layers all over the screen. . . ."

"I don't want to hear any more," she says, putting her hands over her ears. "And I'm going to be one disgruntled lady if we have to sit way on the side or the back row somewhere or right up front." "I know. I'm really glad we came now." "What?" He takes her hands off her ears and says "The movie sounds great and I'm glad I came along. Where'd you hear about it?" "This? I thought everybody knew about it. Big ads. Posters all over town. And these great film buffs at work have been talking about it long before it hit the States and maybe a half-dozen reviews and articles I read, all raves." "Nobody mentioned a thing about it to me and I can never get through movie reviews. My loss I suppose. Good thing I know you."

She puts her head on his shoulder. They turn the corner and get closer to the ticket booth. "Have your money ready please," an usher says. "How much?" he says and the usher says "Four dollars." "For two or a season pass?" and the usher says "Per ticket." "I know, but that's highway robbery, four dollars." "It's because of the high cost of the print or something," a man on line says and he says "That's their problem" and to her "I don't think I'm up to paying four for any movie." "Then I'm going in myself, because look at the line behind us and down the block. Probably most of them for the show after this and they'd give their right arm to take our place." "But it's usually two-fifty here, at the most three." "So go home then," and she opens her shoulder bag. "Next," the usher says and he says to her "All right, put your money back, it's big sport all the way tonight," and shoves a ten-dollar bill through the window, holds up three fingers to the cashier and gets a pair of raised eyebrows, two tickets and change.

They go in. "Candy?" "Let's just find seats," she says. There are few seats left and none together it seems and it also seems more people are looking for seats than there are seats. "We're going to be out if we don't split up fast," she says. "There's two," he says, pointing to two seats with clothing on them and a woman sitting between them. "Excuse me, Miss," he says, "but if those seats aren't taken, would you mind moving over one either way so we can sit together?" "I like the one I'm in," the woman says, "no tall heads in front like the free two. As to whose these coats are," taking her own off one of the seats, which still left coats and sweaters on both empty seats, "maybe the people on the other side or behind me know, but not me." The houselights begin fading. She says "You sit in the first seat you get and I'll find one on my own." "Wait. Maybe these two aren't taken and we can sit a seat apart from each other," but she's already down the aisle. He yells into the row "Excuse me, you people in there. Is one of the seats with the coats on them not being reserved?" The whole row except the three people sitting beside the empty seats look at him. He finds a seat two rows back. He looks around where she might be sitting and sees her in the third row or so, moving past several people to get to a seat. "Pardon me, pardon me, pardon me," she seems to be saying. The movie begins.

It ends. There's quite a lot of applause for a movie and in a theater that's not known for being patronized by cinemaphiles. Not a very good picture though, he thinks. The houselights go on. Most of the audience get up to leave. He doesn't see her where she was sitting before. Maybe the row became too close for her and she changed seats during the movie. He makes his way up the aisle. "I don't get it," a man in the aisle says and the woman with him says "What can I tell you? If it had any faults, complexity certainly wasn't one of them." "It isn't I don't understand it. It was a travesty." "So? Suddenly travesties can't be profound?" "I mean it was stupid, juvenile, ridiculous. It ridiculed our intelligence it was so jejune and dumb." "Let's just say we have different opinions about that." "Let's say that for sure," one of the three young men behind them says. "Okay, then one of you explain to me its meaning and appeal," the man says to them, "because outnumbered like this, maybe I'll admit I didn't get it after all." "Explain it in just one quick shot up the aisle?" the younger man says. "Let's save it for outside when we're not getting so pinched and pushed," the woman says. "Good idea," the man says, "we can talk about it over coffee or beer. You guys game? I am. Enid?" "Yes," the woman says. "Why not," one of the younger men says.

He waits for her in the lobby. Just as many people seem to be waiting in line to see the movie as leaving the theater. She doesn't show. The doors open on the other side of the lobby and the waiting line moves in. The doors the people who were leaving came out of are shut and he tries but can't open them from the lobby. He climbs over the rope that separates the two lines and goes back to the theater and looks around for her. Almost every seat is filled and again more people seem to be looking for seats than there are seats. He goes down to the first few rows where she was sitting before. "Bud? Up here." She's about halfway up the aisle, sitting right in the middle of the theater. There's an empty seat next to her with her coat on it. "Joan, what are you doing? Aren't you leaving?" "I want to see it again, all right with you? I didn't see you leave but thought you'd figure out my plans and come back. I didn't want to lose these two seats together." "I'm not staying a second time." A man behind Bud says to her "That seat taken?" "Bud?" "Yes," he says to the man, "she was holding it for me," and moves into the row, hands her her coat and sits down. "You have to be kidding," he says, "because never was a movie more overrated in my life. What's so worth sitting a second time around for?" "Everything. Acting, directing, editing, screenplay and God knows what else." "What do you know about editing?" "I can tell. The way the film was cut. More. The quick cutting, intercutting, beautifully spliced sequences and frames. Animation into reality and back again and the superimposition of those two and splitscreening and the sound editing too. Tripling and quadrupling the sound track with voice overlays and overlays of previous overlays. It moved so quickly, the whole film. You saw it. That surely had to do with both types of editing and lots of other cinematic stuff that I'm of course not aware of. Hundred-twenty-two minutes running time that felt like half an hour." "For me it was like ten half-an-hours. Twenty." "If you think you'll be bored seeing it again, leave. Really. Go home or for coffee and pick me up after the show if you want or I can take the bus. No problem." "But I want to stay with you now that we finally got two seats together. Whose hand am I going to hold in the coffee shop, mine?" "If you stay, don't grumble, will you? I want to enjoy it."

The houselights fade. A little applause. This time the film is preceded by a preview. "I want to see that when it comes here," she says and he says "I heard it's a bomb." "You said you never read reviews." "Someone told me. Two people in fact. Not buffs but in the buff." "Come on." "It's true. At the Y, in the sauna." "Well I heard it's great." "The editing, acting, writing, directing, sounding, coloring and the rest, I know." "God, you're cynical. You didn't want to stay, why did you?" "Quiet please," a woman behind them says. "I guess what it comes down to is I just don't like movies," he whispers to her. "Shh," she says. "Will you two please be quiet," the same woman says. "It was only me speaking this time," he says, turning around, "and besides, it's only the previews." "It's a trailer of a movie I'm particularly interested in seeing," the woman says, "and a very interesting trailer if you gave it half a chance." "Oh please, what are you talking about, making this trivial commercial movie ad into a major art form." "Do you want me to get the usher?" "Bud, turn around and be quiet." "Excuse me," he says to the woman. "I'm sorry. It is a well-done trailer and truly artistic" and sits back in his seat and Joan says "Good, at least you didn't slug her. Now let's just enjoy the movie." "Will you two can it already," a man

behind them says, "the picture's on." "Only the credits," Bud says and
someone in the same row as him says *shush* and he looks over to the
shushing person and sees a woman with her finger over her lips and the
man next to her nodding at him.

The movie begins. "Hello," a man's voice says, on the black screen,
then just a pair of small moving lips on the black screen, then two lips as
the movie continues, both on the black screen saying *hello*, then three,
four and five lips, all saying hello, and the audience loving it, laughing,
saying "Fantastic . . . too much," some applause, six, seven and eight
lips, then the entire screen quickly taken over by lips, a hundred, two
hundred lips, all looking like different people's lips, male and female
and children's lips, even a few gorilla or some kind of anthropoid or
monkeys' lips, all saying *hello*, though not necessarily at the same time,
when the screen goes black, no lips and suddenly just a pair of lips in
the middle of the screen, which opens wider and gets larger till it takes
over almost the entire screen and these lips growing two short legs with
knobby knees and big feet and after doing a quick softshoe routine,
walking off the screen saying *hello, hello, hello* as it goes, leaving behind
the mouth's tongue in the middle of the screen, a wagging, fluttering
and then gagging tongue, which sends most of the audience into hys-
terics and applause, Joan included, the man behind them kicking Bud's
seat he's breaking up so much, then the tongue licking the black screen
around it white till the entire screen except for the tongue is white and
then licking itself till the screen is nothing but white for a few seconds,
when the story begins. A single bed appears on the white screen, then
disappears and a double bed appears. Then walls, furniture, floor,
paintings, ceiling, all sort of flashing on the screen but staying there.
Then a door in the wall and a doorknob and the doorknob turns and a
man and woman enter the room through the door and sit on the bed. She
puts on stockings, he a pair of different-colored socks. She puts on several pairs of stockings one over the other in increasingly rapid speed and
he several pairs of socks, all different colors and sizes. They hear a door
knock when they're trying to get on their third pair of shoes. "Hello,"
a man's voice behind the door says, the same voice that opened the
movie. "It's him," she says. "No, her," the man on the bed says. "No
him?" "Him her." "Him her she?" "Her his he." "Jest opium," she

says. "He ha who," the voice behind the door says. "Who he has?" she says. "Just injun I think," the voice behind the door says. "Oh what's the dif for angst?" she says; "come in then." The sound of a whistling and hooting audience comes from the screen. The theater audience responds with whistles and hoots. The couple on the screen get up and bow, then throw the shoes they were trying to get on at the camera and Bud ducks, for suddenly that sequence is in 3-D. The door disappears and a man crawls through a large painting of the outdoors, which for a moment had moving birds and clouds in it, rolls his eyes and says "Eye ya, folks, and hello." "Hello," people in the audience and on the audience soundtrack say. "Muh-ruh-puh and luh tongue too, fuhtykes." At the bottom of the screen while he's saying this the words read "*Soustitres*," then "Subtitles," then "Lights, camera, action!" He takes off his coat and underneath is a spangly dress. He lets down his hair to his waist and his body is shaped something like a thin shapely woman's. "Is that a woman or man," Bud whispers to Joan, "or is it not important?" and she says "Shh, I'm enjoying." "Oh, closing hello," the couple say in unison. The woman-man jumps on the bed and they all start tearing at each other's clothes, hose and shoes till they're all nude, the woman-man never exposing the front part of his body as the other two do.

"I'm afraid I'm bored," Bud says to Joan. The screen trio have become a fidgeting, shifting mound under the blanket, making no sounds now but ouches, grunts and shouts. Part of the audience soundtrack is booing and snoring and a few of them chant "We want our money back . . . lynch the producer." The real audience is laughing and applauding, and when the mound grows to the size of about ten to twenty people under the blankets, parts of both audiences yell "More, more." "I'm leaving," Bud says. "Quiet," the man behind him says. "Now . . . oh nothing. Enjoy the unenjoyable. The deplorable. The I-don't-know-whatable. Just enjoy." "How can I do any of those with you yakking all the time?" "Why don't you say something to the people shouting and clapping?" Bud says. "That's different. I'm sure you know the difference." "This is where I came in, Joan. You coming?" "I'll meet you after," she says.

"Excuse me, excuse me please," he says to the row as he leaves. "Why didn't you think of that before?" a woman says. "Don't worry, I'm not going out for what you think. It's only for a few bags of popcorn and soda and I'll be right back." "Can't wait." "You giving up that seat?" a woman says, rushing down the aisle. "Yes." "Pardon me," she says, getting into the same row he came out of, the seat he vacated. People are standing at the back of the theater and crowded at the end of the aisles watching the movie. "Oh my God, they're eating it," someone says. All are laughing. One man covers his eyes.

He gets a beer at a bar, buys a paperback at a bookstore, reads part of it in a fast food place where he has onion rings and tea. The first story's about a man who "once and for all, decided to find out whether he was actually going to be a survivor or victim of this impersonalized and a-lienated industrial society" by sitting at a busy city intersection during a cold spell for a few days, without food or drink. Nobody offered him anything but advice. "Find a job . . . clean yourself . . . go back to India . . . get something to eat." "The civil authorities finally took notice of him" and Klaus died in an ambulance on the way to the hospital. "This story," the author says in a postscript, "is based on a true event that occurred in West Germany several years ago during its greatest modern economic boom. The gentleman in true life happened to be a very successful and talented writer of television documentaries on the physically and mentally afflicted, but for my own unknowable, though I hope not objectionable, reasons, I made him intensely religious, creatively impoverished, and monetarily poor."

He gets up. Skip her. She's a big girl. Let her go home alone. "You like to read?" "Mucho." "Then here's a book you might like." The busboy begins reading the first story. Bud walks downtown, goes into a twenty-five-cent peepshow place just to see what it's like. Filthy. Fetid. Signs on the wall saying "Please don't piss in the booths. It's unsanitary and some of us have holes in our shoes." There are about twenty booths. Above each one is an obscene photograph and the title of the movie being shown. His has a naked woman hugging a big sheepdog. A man's behind the woman. The handwritten caption underneath says "Just in from Sweden: Reddest stuff yet about knockout blonde and a dog with one like King Kong and does he get his? No, she does!" He sticks a quarter in the slot and looks into the viewer. A man on the small screen spends the first minute of the movie rubbing his finger in a jar of Vaseline. Longshots of the man, closeups of his finger in the jar and then just the jar. A woman comes in the room, gives him a big kiss hello, drops her skirt, kicks off her panties, gets down on her knees and he applies the Vaseline to the woman from behind. There are foreign words for subtitles but they're being shown backwards. He can't figure that out since the movie is running forwards. The movie is about three minutes long and ends with the man still applying Vaseline to the woman while unzipping his fly. During the movie men pass his booth and look in through the space where the door won't close. He thinks about sticking in another quarter to see what happens to the couple and Vaseline jar, but the smell inside the booth is too much and so are the eyes that keep looking in.

He leaves the booth. "Go right in," a man says. "No loitering around. Plenty to see. Three booths right there are free. Oriental films and exotic filmstrips upstairs. Postcards and telescopes as souvenirs over here." Leaves the peepshow. Thinks of sitting through an hour or two of a seven-hour all-night porno festival for three dollars across the street, takes a subway back uptown. Joan's standing in front of the theater, talking to a woman. "Where were you? Bud, this is Holly." "Hi." "Hello, Bud." "We were just discussing the movie. Holly's seen it sixteen times." "Seventeen, I think. I don't ever expect to see a better movie, more experimental and real and superincredible and everything else exceptional in every way all at the same time. Not ever. *Children of Paradise* even. Not even *Citizen Kane* or *Les Enfants* Cocteau. You know the one. Or even *8½*, which up till this moment I thought the best. I can never believe what I saw and then see each successive time. I think I might even see it tomorrow night. Yes." "I'll meet you if you don't mind. Bud didn't like it. Twice. Hated it, right?" "It was a big put-on." "I don't see how you can say that." "Bud says a lot of things to be outrageous." "Look, I just went to a twenty-five-cent peepshow downtown—" "That's more your style." Holly laughs. Holly, he now realizes, is the woman who got his seat beside Joan that last time. "Wait a second, Joan. It's not a question of being more my style or to bring it up as any form of comparison. I only wanted to see one once in my life, and you know what? We could have saved ourselves the eight bucks and two hours for that *Big Mouth and Other Things*." "*The Big Mouth and Udder*

Flings." "Swings, I thought," Holly says. They all look at the marquee. "*Swings*. Okay. My mistake. But it wasn't much different from that garbage downtown for a quarter." "From put-on to peepshow. I'd say you've had quite the visual night though haven't come a long way." "But you still can't compare the two types of movies," Holly says, "even if you say, a bit unconvincingly for me, that you're not comparing them aesthetically or any otherwise." "What do you say we forget it for now and go somewhere for a bite." "Right now I don't want to do anything but talk about that movie, and you know for the next hour you're not going to be anything but a sourpuss and a drag." "That's not true." "It has been, Bud." "And you're not being very nice. Maybe I'm not either. As for Holly, well she seems reasonable, but who can ultimately tell? But I'll see you both. Bye bye, have fun." He kisses Joan, shakes Holly's hand. "Nice meeting you." "Same here," Holly says. "See my smile, Joan? Not sour." "I see." The women walk away. "Is he really your husband?" Holly says. "My husband." "Her husband," Bud yells.

He goes home, turns on the TV. Movie about miscegenation and rape, abortion and murder. Same uninteresting movie that was beginning in the bar before and which none of the drinkers took their eyes off of except to reach for their cigarettes and steins. Then a commercial about a bad-tasting mouthwash. Several more awful ads and promos and an announcement that the movie's conclusion will follow station identification, and then two more commercials and a promo and the movie again. He turns the television off. One day I'm going to throw this set out the window. No I won't. Someone below might get hurt.

He goes to bed. He doesn't know what time, but much later Joan comes home. He hears the door shut, then smells toast. She comes into the bedroom. With the light on in the hallway, he watches her undress, put on her pajama top, hears her gargle, brush her teeth, flick the light off, get in bed. "I'm up," he says. "Oh, hi. It's very late, Bud. Goodnight." "Don't you want to talk?" "Not now. Tomorrow." "I'd like to talk now." "And I want to sleep. I also think what we should talk about we should talk about tomorrow." "Let's talk about it now." "All right." She turns on the light. "I think, for the time being, that we've had it, Bud, and should separate." "Divorce is more like it." "No, not divorce, separate. Don't jump to worse than it is. I'll get my own place for half a year or maybe a full year and you can stay here." "Because of one movie?" "It's a long continuation of things. The movie incident was just one of them." "What incident?" "Incidents. Everything. You're just so inflexible and unrelaxed. It's too unrelaxing being with such an unrelaxed man who won't change. But about that movie, you mock it but it opened up something very new for me in the way of living and thinking, more than any group or wise doctor or religious person ever had." "Bull." "See? You won't even ask what. You just say bull. That's you all over, hardly ever interested in what I have to say in depth." "I am interested. Say it." "Not now." "I'm sorry. Please say it. You just can't come in here and say we should separate and call me eternally pigheaded and rigid and blame most of it on a movie and then not explain why you think that movie changed your life. Just tell me. I won't say a word till you're through and probably not even then." "All right. As I said, it didn't change my life as much as open new things up. Its ideas on women and men and relationships and sex. On the sometimes absurdity of living together as couples and the possibility of undiscovered courage and different life styles. It almost documented, as if it knew us, what's been wrong with our personalities together and relationship since its inception, things I've thought about but which that movie made much clearer to me and confirmed. Of the voices we hear. Not so much that. The movie said to me that if your present life is too confining and frustrating and unsatisfactory for reasons you've so far unsuccessfully tried to bring to light, then go out and discover life, that's what. Don't wait for the answers to come from the people and sources that have been most faithful and helpful to you till now, that too. In other words, what it said with that image of the woman feverishly digging around with her hands in the desert and the numerals falling off her watch and then out of her eyes was don't keep looking for water where you've already found there's a ninety-six percent chance there's nothing there but dry sand. You're more a delayer, the movie said, and will be one till you definitely decide to undo your particular personality type, which is hard but not impossible. I'm not a delayer, the movie said, and I'll be less of one—I mean, we're both of everything but you'll be less a delayer and me more the doer if I take advantage of my type and break what's holding me back and not be worried about what I can't so far fathom about my life. I see that as a separation from you and possibly my job and going out and really discovering life, which is maybe as deep as I have to fathom or anybody can. So I'm separating from you and going out and really discovering life. The enriching, fulfilling, powerful, sensual, multidimensional, interesting and creative life in all things and me. The life which at the end of one's life no matter what age as an adult you die one can say was worth living, the person living it or who lived it can say, even if she dies quote too early unquote. Life as perpetual curiosity and recurring passion and joy, and right now it isn't that way with either of us separately or together in almost every way. I'm sorry. And the second time I saw it that meaning became even clearer to me. And after speaking to Holly—well it's obvious she's gained from her sixteen to seventeen viewings of it as many insights and insights in insights about her life and outsights she also says, that her whole life has changed." "Oh please. What's she done since she first saw that movie other than see it fifteen or sixteen more times?" "No, you don't understand." She shuts the light. He begins crying. "Oh come on. Stop it. I won't accept it. Not as a way out or in," she says. "Don't you see? Just that crying proves in some way that life the way you delay it is getting you down too, and you know it'll only get worse for us if we don't separate. What do you think all those flashing yesses in every language were when that woman was all skin and thirst and bone and the sun was at its highest and so hot? That was positiveness. Affirmation and hope. That she could do it. Get up, it said. Upsy-daisy and no clothes on, no energy—hell, she did it anyway: crawled, smiled, masturbated, roared, walked and ran on. Then an oasis and one not even on a map. A little Eden, that water hole. That could be it for you and me. Edens all over the place. It sounds ridiculous but it's not. And this time I'm not going to feel sorry or sentimental or any of that for your crying and what we once were and have come to and so forth, and you should be happy about that. We have all the signs and they pinpoint the way for us and almost tell us how far we have to go. That was the point of those almost subliminal shots of landmarks and milestones, but we still continue not to want to know or see them and go off in the wrong direction when we—" He gets out of bed, unplugs the television set, opens the window wide and takes a deep breath. "What are you doing?" "Throwing the television out." "Put it down. That's my

TV." "We both got it for our marriage." "My sister gave it to us for our marriage so it's more mine than yours." "Hello down there," he yells, "anybody in the backyard?" "Don't you dare." She gets out of bed and turns the light on. "I'm going to drop something very heavy and possibly lethal from one of the apartments to the backyard of One-fifteen West Seventy-third Street, so if anyone's down there in the dark below, let me know." "They might not be able to hear." "Nobody's down there." She tries grabbing the set out of his hands. He drops it out the window, she screams and it crashes below. Windows open, people look out. "Anybody jump?" someone yells. She pulls down the shade and says "You're crazy and also corny with your stupid symbolic gestures worthy of the most insipid soaps," takes her pillow and goes into the next room and slams the door. "I saw Clark Gable do that once," he yells. "Shut up." He feels bad but gets to sleep.

Next morning there's a note on the kitchen table saying "I'm moving in with Holly. For now I don't need much. If I don't stay there permanently and you don't move out of the apartment, then I'm getting my own place. I hope we can arrange this amicably. If you can't, then go off the road again, but I'm not. Please don't destroy the rest of the place till we divvy it up. Cheers."

He takes all her books on movies and movie directors and the Aesthetics of Cinema and so forth and throws them out the window. Then he realizes the mess he's made down there and goes downstairs with a broom and dustpan, gets a garbage can from the basement, goes to the backyard and cleans up the mess, dumps the broken books and television set pieces into the can, carries the can, broken television cabinet and tube to the street. Then he goes to the library and spends a couple of hours there trying to find some books or a book that will lift his spirits and change some of his ways and give him more confidence in this time of emotional and forthcoming emotional stress or at least convince him he doesn't have to have this stress or in some way bear out something of what he thinks his attitudes about life are or just distract him till he feels a lot better than he does now. He goes through the fiction and poetry and literary criticism and philosophy and biography and religion sections but finds nothing. As he's leaving, the librarian whom he's come to know here over the past few years says from behind the counter "Can't find anything you like today?" "Sorry." "There are other branches, or the bookstores—what about one of those?" "Good idea. I'll go to one now." But he was in a bookstore yesterday and to him each library branch is like the next. "See you," he says. She smiles and waves. He goes home depressed.

LAYAWAYS

Mr. Toon says good-bye and goes, keeps the door open for two men who come in. Wasn't a very good sale, pair of socks, layaways for a couple of workshirts. Two men look over the suits.

"Anything I can do for you, fellas?"

"Just looking," shorter one says.

"Harry, mind if I go to the bathroom?" Edna says.

"Why ask? You ask me almost all the time and I always say yes.—You don't see anything you got in mind you're looking for, just ask me. We got things in back or different sizes of those."

"Thank you," same man says.

"Why do I ask?" Edna says. "Because I like to ask. Because I have to ask. Because I'm a child who always has to ask her daddy if she can make."

"You're my wife, talk to me like my wife, not like my child."

"You don't get anything I say. You're so unclever, unsubtle."

"What's that supposed to mean?"

"You don't pick things up."

"I pick up plenty. I picked you up thirty-two years ago, didn't I? One pickup like that, I don't need any more."

"Well that at least is an attempt at cleverness. What I meant," she says lower, "is those two men. I don't want to leave you out here with them alone when I make."

"They're okay."

"I don't like their looks. They're too lean. No smiling. One has sneakers on."

"So they're lean and don't smile. Maybe they got good reason to be."

"They're swift, they do a lot of running, I don't like it."

"They're okay I'm telling you. You work here Saturdays, you think you know everything. But I've been in this neighborhood for how many years now, so I got a third eye for that."

"Your third eye you almost lost in the last holdup."

"Shut up. They might overhear."

17

"And get ideas?"

"And get scared out of here thinking we always get holdups."

"We do get holdups."

"But not always. You want to go to the bathroom, don't be afraid. You got my permission. Go."

"Call Joe out first."

"Joe's on his break."

"Let him take it out here."

"He's taking it in back because he wants to get away from out here.— Sure nothing I can do for you, fellas? You're looking for a suit, sport jacket? Just what size are you exactly?"

"If we see anything, we'll tell you," shorter one says. Taller one's holding a hangered suit to his chest.

"Big one doesn't talk much," Edna says. "He I think we got to be especially leery of."

"You're paranoid, you know what it is?"

"No."

"It means you're paranoid. You know what it is."

"I was just testing to see if you do, and you didn't. You couldn't define it."

"I can too. You're paranoid. *You.* That's my defining it. To every lean-looking man not smiling if he has sneakers on you're paranoid."

"So what's a man with sneakers buying or looking at a suit for?"

"To buy for later. If he buys a suit from us, he'll go to Clyde's or Hazlitt's and buy a pair of shoes to match. He's in a buying mood. These guys, they get a paycheck Friday, they spend it all at once the next day and mostly on liquor and clothes. What do you think you're here for? Leave me alone with your being paranoid. One robbery this month—"

"Two."

"One. That second we didn't know was a robbery."

"The one last week? Call Joe out and let him tell you how much a robbery it wasn't. That was a knife that man pulled out of his newspaper on Joe, big as your head."

"But he was crazy. He carries the knife and makes threats so he can feel like a big man. He does it to lots of stores around here and they just tell him 'Sure, here's a penny, all we got, it was a slow day,' and show him the door."

"Okay, that one doesn't count. But what does? When they stick it in your heart?"

"Shush, will you? They'll hear. You're going to the girls' room, go like I said, but don't worry about bringing out Joe."

"No, I'll stay here. I don't want to leave you alone with them."

"Do what you want."

"At least say thanks."

"Why should I? I don't think you're right."

"My heart's in the right place."

"Okay, your heart. You're a dream. You saved my life. You made me live twenty years younger, oh boy am I lucky. But scare these two away with your knife talk just before my antennas say I'm going to make a big sale with them and I'll be mad as hell at your heart because we need every cent we can get.—That one's a real good buy and a beauty. Want to try it on?"

"Yeah, that's a good idea, where can I?" shorter man says. They come over to the counter Edna's behind and where I've been talking to her and he holds out the suit to me. "How much?"

"Tag's right on the arm cuff. Sometimes they're hard to find. Size forty-four? This is for you? I say that because it's more a size for him. You can't be more than a thirty-six, and besides, this one's a long and you're a regular."

"I'm regular, thirty-six, you're right, you really know your line," and from under the suit he's still holding he points a pistol at me. Other one opens his jacket and aims a sawed-off shotgun at Edna and cocks it. "Don't scream. Whatever you do, don't. You'll both be nice and quiet now, and you call out your friend Joe. But call him out nice and quietly, don't startle him. Just say—"

"I know, I know how to say it," I say.

"Quiet. Listen to me. Just say 'Joe, could you come out and help me with this fitting for a second, please?' Exact words. Got them?"

"Yes."

"Repeat them."

"Joe, could you come out and help—"

"Okay, say it."

"Do as he says," Edna says.

"I will, you think I'm crazy? Joe, could you come out and help me with this fitting for a second with this gentleman, please?"

"I still got ten minutes," Joe says.

"He's a nice boy," Edna says. "He's my son. He's his son. He won't do anything. Don't touch him."

"We just want him out here, lady. Now call him too, same kind of words but harder."

"Joe, will you please come out here a second? Your father—Harry's got two customers at once and it's too much. For a fitting."

"You can't do it?"

"I don't know how like you yet."

"You don't know how. You'll never know how. I worked my butt off on stock today and want to rest. Oh hell," and he comes out holding a magazine and a coffee container.

Taller one holds his shotgun behind him, other one inside the suit.

"Which one needs the fitting?" Joe says.

"Just keep it quiet, baby," shorter one says pulling out the gun and aiming it at Joe. Other one has the shotgun on me, Edna, then keeps it on me.

"Don't hurt him," Edna says about Joe.

"I won't if he does everything we say."

"Everything," Joe says. "Give them it all, Harry."

"You think I won't? Look, gentlemen. Come behind here and take everything, please, take it all. Edna, get out and let them in."

"No, lady, you dish it out for us in one of your stronger bags."

"As you say," she says and rings "No Sale," he looks over the counter into the bill and change tray and says "Okay," and she starts putting the money into a bag. They keep their guns on us, their backs to the store windows. Joe has a gun on the shelf under the cash register but deep in back. He got a permit for it last month because of the three robberies so far this year when each time we got cleaned out. Edna drops a few change rolls and bills on the floor.

"I'll get it," Joe says.

"You'll get nothing," shorter man says. "Pick them up, lady."

"She's too nervous. She went through a robbery here just last week with a guy with a knife."

"I am very nervous," she says.

"Then you pick them up and empty the rest in the bag, but make it quick."

"Just be careful, Joe, and don't do anything silly," I say.

"Like what?" shorter man says.

Man taps on the door, shorter man waves at him, holds up one finger and the man goes.

"Like not making any wrong moves which are innocent but you might think suspicious," I say, "that's all. We're not armed or anything like that, I wouldn't allow it here, and no trip alarms to the police. We'll only cooperate. Do only what they say, Joe, and nothing more."

"I know."

But I can see by his look he doesn't. "Let me get the money."

"Why you want to get it?" taller one says.

"Because Joe seems nervous too. He went through the war. He still has tropical diseases."

"I'm not nervous. I want to give them all the money and for them to leave right away with no trouble."

"Why you two talking like you're up to something?" taller one says.

"We're not," I say.

"They're not," Edna says.

"No, we're not," Joe says.

"What do you have back there?"

"Nothing," Joe says. "Come and look."

"Pick up the money, old man," shorter one says to me. "You come away from there" to Joe. "Go into the middle of the room. You stay back there, lady."

Joe goes to the middle of the room. People pass on the street. Two look our way as they walk and I guess don't see anything but don't hesitate or stop. Radio music from in back is still playing. A dog's barking nearby and from somewhere far off is a fire engine siren. I bend down and pick up the money and put it in the bag and empty the rest of the tray money into the bag and lift the tray and stick the big bills under it into the bag and say "I guess you want our wallets too" and shorter one says "And her pocketbook money and all your watches and rings."

"My purse is under the counter," Edna says. "Can I reach for it?"

"Go ahead."

"You want the personal checks from today too?" I say.

"Forget the checks."

We empty our wallets, watches, rings and purse into the bag and shorter one says "Good, now go in back. The two men, right now. Lady stays here. We're not taking her so don't worry. Just want her standing here between you and us so you don't do anything stupid, now go."

We go in back. Joe looks through the tiny two-way glass to the front he had me install last month. I say "They taking her? What are they doing? Joe?" I hear the door close. Joe runs out and goes behind the counter and gets his gun and yells "Both of you, flat on the floor" and Edna shouts "Don't, let them go" and I shout "Joe, what are you doing?" The men aren't even past the store yet. They're in the street flagging down a cab with that tapping man from before when they see Joe opening the door and turn all the way to him and shorter one fumbles for something in the bag and taller one reaches under his jacket and Joe's yelling "You goddam bastards" and the two from before have their guns out and Joe's shooting the same time they're shooting or almost, I think Joe first, and our windows break and Edna screams and blood smacks me in the face and across my clothes and the two men fall and Edna bounces against the wall behind the counter and falls and glass is sprayed all over the store and clock above me breaks and Edna's jaw looks gone and face and neck a mess and Joe's alive and the tapping man from before gets up from where he dived and starts running across the avenue and Joe fires at him and runs over to the men on the ground and I yell "Joe, stop, enough" and kicks their guns to the curb and runs a few feet after the man and then back to the store and jumps through the empty window and sees his mother on the floor and screams and drops to his knees and says "Mom, Mom" and I hold his shoulders and cry and mutter "Edna, Joe" and he throws my hands off and runs to the front and opens the door and shouts "You bastards" and one of the men on the ground raises his head an inch and people who have come near them now scatter every which way and Joe puts two bullets into the man who raised his head and grabs the pistol and shotgun from the curb and puts the one shotgun round left into the taller man's head he just put two bullets in and about five bullets from the pistol into the already unconscious or just dead shorter man and then he kicks their bodies and whacks the shotgun handle over the shorter man's head and throws the broken gun away and pistolwhips what's left of the taller man's head and gets on his knees and sticks the pistols into his pockets and pounds the ground with his fists and some people come over to him and the bell from the door tells me someone's coming into the store while I get a pain in my chest that shoots from it to all four limbs and sudden blackness in my head that's only broken up by lightning-like cracks and fall on Edna and feel myself going way off somewhere and in my blackness and lightning and going away I feel around for her hand and find it and hold it and pass out from whatever, maybe the chest pain.

I ask to be in the same room with her but they say we have to stay in two different intensive care units at opposite ends of the hall, one for serious gunshot injuries and other for coronaries and strokes and the like. Joe sits by my bed for the five minutes they give him and says "I hope Mom dies, it's not worth it to her or you if she lives. The bullets went—"

Nurse puts her finger over her mouth to him and I nod to Joe I understand.

"How's the store?" I say and he says "I think I better go in tomorrow. We got all those layaways for Easter. The customers will be disappointed last day before the holidays start not to get them and they won't want them after and will want their money back."

"You better go in then."

"I'm not afraid to."

"Why should you be?"

"People say those two men got friends who'll want to get revenge."

"What do the police say?"

"They say what I did will act as a deterrent against revenge and more robberies, but what am I going to be a deterrent with? They took away my permit and gun."

"For the time being?"

"They got to investigate if I couldn't've not used it. But who knows?"

"Don't go in then. I don't want you getting killed."

"But those customers. They got layaways and it's our best two days."

"Do you have to talk about business now?" nurse says to him.

"It's okay," I say. "Store talk relaxes me and I feel all right. Don't go in," I tell Joe. "Go back to college. Stay away from business. I just made up my mind for you."

"I like the business. I got my own family to support too. I want to keep the store."

"We'll get insurance from the robbery and the sale of the merchandise later on. You can have half of it. You deserve it. You have to go back into business, open a store in a quieter neighborhood."

"In a quieter neighborhood the store will die."

"Go into another business."

"What other business I know but men's clothes?"

"Once you know retailing you can open up any kind of store."

"I like men's clothes."

"I don't think your father should be discussing this now," nurse says.

"I feel much better, Miss. Anyway, it wasn't a heart attack I had."

"It was a heart attack."

"It was, Dad."

"It was indigestion. It was that doubled up with nerves. I didn't deserve them? My own wife? Him? That whole scene?"

"You'll have to go," she tells Joe.

"I'll see you later." He kisses my forehead and leaves.

"Could you call him back?" I say.

"It'd be better not to."

"I want to ask him something I never got an answer from. If I don't get that answer I'll be more worried and heartsick than if I do."

She goes outside the room and Joe comes back. "What?" he says.

"You going back to the store?"

"I guess I have to."

"You really aren't afraid?"

"A friend of mine, Nat, has offered to stay with me. He's a big guy and will take care of the register and look after the door."

"Call Pedro also. He called me just a week before the accident and asked if business was going to be good enough to hire him back. Call him. His number's in the top drawer of the counter."

"I know where it is. We have money to pay him?"

"Even if you have to take it out of my pockets. The glass fixed?"

"They put it in yesterday. We had to. Cops didn't want it boarded up if we're going to still occupy it and other store owners complained it looked bad for everybody else."

"They're right. Don't keep more than three hundred dollars in cash there any one time. You get one dollar more, deposit it—it's worth the walk."

"I know."

"I still have to tell you. Two guys like those two come in, even one who looks suspicious, don't take unnecessary risks. No risks, hear me?"

"I won't."

"Give even a ten-year-old boy who's holding up the store whatever he wants."

"A ten-year-old I'm not giving in to."

"If he has a gun?"

"That's different."

"That's what I'm saying. But any older person who says this is a holdup—even if he or she doesn't show a gun, give them what they want. Remember, you're only going back to be nice to the layaways, right?"

"I'm going back because I also need the money, me and my family, you and Mom, and to tell the goddamn thieves they're not shoving me out."

"They know that already. Listen to me, don't be so tough. I can tell you stories about other tough merchants. I'm not saying what you did caused your mother like she is. But if you didn't get so crazy so suddenly, not that you could help it—well right?"

"Don't make me feel bad."

"I'm not trying to."

"Don't blame me because I got excited. Sick as you are, I'm telling you this now for all time."

"I understand you. In your own way that day, you did okay."

He waves.

"Where you going? Give your father a kiss good-bye. He needs it."
He kisses my lips. He never did that before. I also never asked him to
kiss me any time before. My own father asked me to kiss him hundreds
of times and I always did. But only once on his lips did I kiss him and
that was a few minutes after he died. I start to cry. Joe's gone. Nurse asks
me what's wrong. "Got any more news on my wife?"

"You know we're not allowed to speak about her."

"What am I supposed to think then, she's dead?"

"She's not. Your son told you. She's holding her own."

"She isn't much, right?"

"I can't say. She also has the best equipment to help her. You can talk
about it more tomorrow with her doctors when they move you to a semi-
private."

I'm released three weeks later and go back to the store a month after
that. Joe's had another robbery. He gave them what he had without a
fuss. Pedro was there that day and later said he'd never let anyone take
anything from him again, even if it wasn't his store. Pedro got a gun.
Two of the merchants on the street stood up for him for the gun permit.
Because Joe's not allowed to apply for one again for two months, he told
the police Pedro needed the gun to take the store receipts to the bank.
Pedro keeps the gun in back. He told Joe it's no good keeping it under
the counter or in the register for where's the first place they look? They
find it, they just might use it on you. He's been robbed three other times
besides his twice at our store and in back's where they always send you
or want to either tie you up or lock you in the men's room so they have
as much time as they can to get away.

Edna's in the nursing home now paralyzed from the neck down. Even
if she comes out of her coma she'll be paralyzed like that for life. She'll
never be able to speak and if she gets out of the coma she'll hardly be able
to think. She should've died in the hospital or in the store but more in
the hospital because there's more dignity to dying there. The doctors
say she won't last another few months. So I go back to the store just to
get my mind off her and have something to do, though my own doctor
says I shouldn't. I say hello to Pedro and he says "I'm really sorry what
happened to you, Mr. Sahn."

"It was a long time ago."

"It's never a long time for something like that and it's still happening with your wife, right?"

"Maybe it isn't too long ago at that. But you've been a great help to my son and me and if we could afford it, we'd double your hourly salary and also put you on for all six days."

"I'm glad I got what I got, so don't worry."

"But we'll give you forty cents more an hour starting today."

"Hey Pop," Joe says, "what are you trying to do, rob us? We haven't got forty cents more to give."

"Twenty cents will be fine," Pedro says, "and I can really use it."

"Twenty then," I say.

I go to work every other day and on Saturday of that same week two men come in when Pedro and I are reading different sections of the newspaper and Joe's taking care of the one customer in the store. The men take out their guns before the door's even closed and thinner one points his at Pedro and me and heavier one at the customer and Joe and says "Holdup, nobody go for anything or step on alarms." Customer says "Oh my God" and Pedro says "We freeze, fellas, no worry about that, we're no dopes" and heavier one goes to the register and starts emptying it into a briefcase and thinner one says to me "You there, owner, hold this" and gives me another briefcase and says "Your wallet and everything else in it and get the same from the rest" and we all dump our wallets and watches and rings in it, but I don't have a ring because mine was taken the last time and for some reason never recovered though everything else in the bag outside was. Heavier one comes around the counter and runs in back and comes out and says "They got no storerooms to lock themselves in and the bathroom has no door" and says to us "All right, you all go in back but way in back and don't come out for five minutes minimum or I swear one does you all die" and Pedro says "Don't worry, we've been through this before and we all go in back for ten minutes not five, I'll see to that" and we go in back and Joe goes to the two-way and says "They've left" and Pedro reaches behind a pile of shirt boxes and pulls out a gun and I drop the phone receiver and say "Pedro, don't" and he says "I'm not letting them get away with it, Mr. Sahn, I told your son" and the customer sticks all his fingers into his mouth and says "Oh no, oh no" and Joe says "Let me have the gun" and Pedro says "No, I'm licensed for it and get in trouble letting anyone else use it" and Joe says "But I know how to use it" and Pedro says "I know too, the police showed me one day in practice" and Joe says "One day? You crazy? Let me have it" and I say "None of you, let them go, nobody goes after them" but Joe reaches for the gun and Pedro shouts "Watch out, it's cocked" and jerks it back before Joe can get hold of it and the gun goes off and bullet into Pedro's chest and we hear shots from outside and windows breaking and duck to the floor, customer already there bawling, and Joe yells "You goddamn bastards" and grabs the gun and runs to the front but the men had only shot out the windows because I suppose they thought they were being shot at by us and by the time Joe gets to the street they're in a car and gone.

I close the store and sell the entire stock, Joe goes back to pharmacy college for the next year with me paying all his bills, Pedro dies from the bullet through his lungs, Edna lives on in a coma for another month before she succumbs in her sleep the doctors say, I have another heart attack and move South into a single room by myself among a whole bunch of much older people in the same crummy hotel, living off my social security and Edna's life insurance and our savings and maybe not in a better hotel till Joe graduates and can earn a salary large enough not only for his family but to begin paying me back. Then I get a phone call from his sister-in-law who says Joe got in an argument in the park with three men who were mugging a young couple and they beat him in his kidneys and head till he was dead.

I return for the funeral and because I don't like the South much with all that sun and beach and older people having nothing to do but wait for death and me with them, I move back for good and open another store, but a much smaller one for candies and greeting cards and things like that in a much safer neighborhood. I ask Joe's wife Maddie if she and her kids want to share an apartment with me to save money and because I'd also like to be with them more and she says "Actually, I don't want to, not that I don't like you, Dad. But with us not having much money and all and the kids for the time being so small, maybe for the next four years and if I don't get remarried or move in with some guy, it's probably the best of ideas."

So we live like that, me not making much in my store in a neighborhood that only rarely has a robbery, my grandchildren asking me questions and wanting me to play with them like I'm their dad, Maddie working part-time and going out with different men and sometimes staying overnight in their apartment, but not really being attracted to any of them just as I think they're not attracted to her. Some days we go to the two graves in the plot for eight I bought thirty years ago and that's the only time we all just hold one another, the kids not understanding it too much, and say some prayers from a little book the cemetery provides and cry and cry.

SMALL BEAR

Susan comes out to the porch and says "The most amazing thing just happened by the road. I was picking raspberries, there aren't many yet so most went into my mouth, when a man, oh, about fifty or so, stopped his car and said from the front seat 'Excuse me, lady, but have you seen any sign of small bear?' "

"A small bear?"

"Just 'small bear' he said, no 'a.' "

"I know, but you never told me anything about—"

"I never heard of any around here either. But he said a small one, probably not much older than a cub, was hit by a car at the sharp right by the Palette place—"

"Which sharp right is that? The one heading to the point or to town?"

"The Palette place is the next property over on the way to the point. You never saw the name on their mailbox all the times you jogged past?"

"How many times have I? We've been here five days and I alternate my route every other. Either I wasn't looking or was but with too much sweat in my eyes or I forgot. But what about the bear? Was it killed?"

"No, that's what he meant. It was hit, or more likely just stunned by the car—not his but the man who caretakes for Olgrin's—and it limped into the woods on our side. You sure you're interested?"

"Sure I am."

"Then why'd you look at your book? It seemed you were still reading or wanting to."

"I was checking the page number so I could close the book and listen to you finish your story. I still didn't catch the page number. I'm not being rude, but hold it." I look at the book. Page fifty-six. I close the book and look at her. "Okay."

"How is it?"

"You know: the same thing. Moscow. Mikvahs. The Actors' Club. People with hair in their ears and funny noses. Entertaining but nothing great. You don't have to go out of your way to read it."

"I'd always read anything she wrote. Even if you said it was absolutely awful, which you usually do about everybody's books."

"The bear. The baby bear."

"A little more than a cub, though weighing around a hundred pounds." She pushes aside my feet and sits at the end of the chaise lounge I'm on, takes my juice glass off the porch deck and sips at it and puts it down. "He said it's probably all right and not to worry. If it's only slightly hurt, it'll take care of itself. If it was hit bad by the car, it'll stay away from us because it's frightened of people whether it's sick or well. But can you imagine? A man stopping a car—I thought, to ask me directions—and saying first thing have I seen any sign of small bear? When he told me his name, I realized his family had been on this peninsula for over two hundred years."

"Well, I don't know much about Northeastern wildlife, but I do think that cubs of all breeds of bear travel with their parents—at least with their mothers—till they're almost adults. And also that when they're injured, or maybe that's just full-grown adults—"

"I asked him that too. When they're hurt, don't they get crazy and attack people? He said they rarely go crazy and usually only when they're desperately hungry or feverish with a bear disease."

I sit back, look at the sky and say almost to myself "Bears in these woods."

"You don't like the idea?"

"No, I love it. Bears and deer we saw the other day and shrews, whatever they are, and loons crooning to one another from different coves and all kinds of life like that. Maybe even wolves and elk."

"Wolves I never saw in all my summers here and elk, or moose, are further north. Bears, nobody I know has ever heard of around here, but I guess they can get lost. Want some tea?"

"No thanks. Too hot out here as it is."

"I'll make it iced."

"Really, sweetheart, I'm very content. I'll just pull the lounge into the shade."

"Then that's my forest report for this hour." She squeezes my knee, gets up and goes into the living room and sits at the desk where she's translating the poems of a contemporary Hungarian poet never translated into English. I open my book to page fifty-six.

An hour later, when I'm in the bedroom typing a letter to my sons about the bear incident and my stay here, I hear Susan screaming. I run downstairs and out the front door. She's not there and is no longer screaming. "Susan," I yell. "Susan, Susan." She screams again. It's from the back. I run through the living room to the porch and yell from it "Susan, what's wrong? Where are you?"

"Over here. Please. I've been mauled. Quick. Help me. It's still around."

"I'm coming—wait," and I run inside, grab the axe off the log pile and run outside and down the porch steps and into the woods where she's still screaming. About a hundred feet from the house, in a small clearing, I see her lying on the grass, no clothes on, on a blanket, book and clothes and mosquito repellent bottle beside her, her arms raised to me, smiling and saying "I was only kidding. I wanted to get you here fast. What took you so long? It's obvious you don't love me anymore."

"I went for the axe."

"You do love me. It's obvious. You were going to kill the bear for me."

"I was going to if it was attacking you, or at least would have tried, but I mostly just wanted to chase it away with this."

"So it could come back and try to kill me a second time?"

"Susan, there was no bear. And if you have to know, I don't see myself hitting anything with an axe, blunt or sharp side, but would have if either of us was in danger."

"Sit down. Lie down. Take your clothes off. You're making me feel twenty degrees warmer with your flannel shirt on. Make love to me."

"It was chilly upstairs. With all those tall trees, that room never gets warm."

"Make love to me she asked."

I sit down and take off my shirts and sneakers and socks.

"The pants."

"The pants," I say. I take off my pants and undershorts. We hold one another. She smells from the repellent lotion. I kiss her chest and say "What would we really do if we saw the bear—from a distance I mean."

"I asked that man. He said to call the game warden."

"You shouldn't have scared me like that."

"I felt I had to because you never seem to get scared or excited about anything anymore. You've also been staying away from me up here and you've been practically mute."

"That's almost true. I have. I came to Maine to rest and I suppose I'm doing nothing but resting. Maybe because I've nothing much to do but read and write letters. I don't sail. I don't garden. I don't like to sightsee. I've already collected enough rocks and seashells to fill a valise. But I promise that from now on I'll be a physical dynamo, cutting down old trees and turning them into firewood and going everywhere you want to and whatever else you want and also a chatterbox."

I kiss her and we begin to make love. She's on top of me now and I'm looking up at her holding her arms when her head snaps to the side to look at something it seems she heard in the woods. Then I hear it, something heavy stumbling, walking, falling down, rolling over it seems, getting up, stumbling and walking again.

"It's the bear," she shouts and she gets off me and runs through the woods in the opposite direction of the noise and then I hear her running up the porch steps and the screen door slam.

I'm standing now, axe in my hand, and am about to run, but look into the woods. Maybe it's one of the Palettes or a lost or hiking houseguest or a clammer coming up from our cove for something or a deer or big dog. It's a small black bear about as big as a medium-sized dog and it's walking toward me. Then it's in the clearing with me, stops, bites at its back, I guess to get some bugs away, looks at me, growls a moment but not loudly and shows a little of its big teeth, and falls over and doesn't move.

I stand there, not knowing what to do. If I run or sneak away quietly it might get up and chase me. If I stay frozen it might think I'm harmless and walk past me or turn around and go back into the woods, and if it didn't and started to come at me, I'd at least be facing it and could try to protect myself with the axe. But it just lies there. It doesn't seem to be breathing. Some bugs have collected on its head. I pick up a twig and throw it at the bear. The twig lands a few inches from its face and the bear doesn't move. I lob several pinecones at it before one hits its shoulder. It doesn't move. I walk closer to it. Its eyes are closed. I touch its back with the tip of a long branch and jump back. It doesn't move. There's wet and dried blood on its body and a strong animal smell coming off it. I shake its back with the blunt end of the axe and then jump away. It doesn't move other than for my shaking it. I'm almost sure it's dead.

"Stan, where are you?" Susan yells from the house.

"It's okay. I'm coming." I gather our clothes, lotion, book and blanket and run to the house. Susan's behind the screen door, dressing, and says "Get in here. What happened? I called the game warden. I thought you'd been attacked or were up a tree."

"The bear's already dead, I think. I shook and shook it and it wouldn't move." I start putting on my clothes.

"You shook it with your hands?"

"It's small. And with the axe. Though first it looked kind of sickly at me and then plopped over unconscious and never budged again."

"The warden said if it is a cub, then it got lost from its mother at least a hundred miles from here and would be the first authentic reporting of a bear in this area in nearly twenty years. You know, the strangest thing is I never believed that Mr. Riverdore's story about it being hit by a car. I thought he was only telling me it to stimulate my interest in him in a Maine woods sort of way."

"Then why'd you tell me the story after you came back from the road?"

"Because it was a good story. I know a good one when I hear it—I teach the damn things—and that one seemed too good not to pass on. Besides, just before he stopped me, I was trying to concoct some kind of tale to get us to make love in the woods, which I knew with all the bugs around and a dozen other excuses you wouldn't want to, and that one fit in perfectly. It worked, didn't it?"

"We never completed it."

"Maybe after the game warden goes, but upstairs."

"You didn't really call him, did you? Because that was no bear down there. It was a deer."

"Oh come on. I saw it."

"You only heard it."

"Only heard it, but it was a bear. I know it was, just by the scared way you ran back here."

"I ran that way because the mosquitoes were biting the hell out of me."

"Where were you bitten?" She starts unbuttoning my shirt. I push her hands off.

"On my backside. Legs. Leave me alone. And if there was a bear, how come one of those two men didn't call the game warden before you?"

"Maybe they didn't think it important enough to tell the warden, or were looking around for it first before they called. I don't know. They're local people, live around wildlife all their lives. Maybe they wanted to have some fun shooting or trapping it and then call."

"Please. You didn't believe that Mr. Riverdore's story but you believe mine?"

"He I believed was just trying to attract me with the story, which it turns out he wasn't, or maybe he was, but with a real story, while you . . . well now I'm not sure. Come on, tell me. Did you see a bear there or not? If you didn't, then I have to call the game warden to save him the trip out here."

"There was no bear. It was a very big deer, maybe a moose, but it ran away."

She picks up the phone receiver and starts dialing.

"No, I'm joking. It was a bear all right, but it didn't die. It walked away."

She puts down the receiver.

"No, it didn't walk or run away. It's dead, or seemed to be when I left it. I poked it with the axe as I said. Flies were already on it, though maybe they also do that when it's resting or asleep."

"Why are you telling me all these stories? Which is it? Bear or not or dead or not or what?"

"What I just said. Bear. Dead. And why all the stories? To pay you back for scaring the hell out of me with your screams and then for nearly getting me killed with that bear."

"With a cub? You could have danced with it."

"Scratched then, I could have been seriously scratched. It was over a hundred pounds, and who knows what bacteria they might have on their nails."

"A little iodine and you would have lived. And you proved yourself the big hero when I bet you didn't even know you were or as much, rushing into the woods to kill it or chase it away, so you should be grateful to me for that. Stop pretending you're a baby," and she motions me with her finger to come to her. I do and we hug just as a car drives up. It's the game warden. He gets out of his van with a rifle. We meet him in front of the house and tell him the story, but say we were in the woods looking for dead wood to chop up when we first heard the sound of the bear.

"Show me where you left it," he says, "but stay a ways behind me."

We walk to the clearing, the game warden with his rifle cocked. The bear's not there.

"He was probably injured and feeling defenseless and playing dead till you left," he says.

"Or maybe you didn't see the bear after all," Susan says to me.

"Susan, what a stupid thing to say. Not only are you going to get me in trouble with this man, but would I have let you bring him out here if I hadn't seen the bear?"

"I don't think so."

"I'm sure you wouldn't," the game warden says. "But if you did, it would be an extremely dangerous prank, as that bear could be on the loose around someone else's house and I can't be reached now since I'm away from my car."

"I swear I saw the bear," I say. "It came out of the woods right there, fell down right here and never moved again. It had blood on its body. Maybe some spilled on the ground."

He bends down and looks. "I don't see any."

"But there definitely was a bear hit by a car?" Susan says.

"Oh yeah. Man who hit it called me right after you did and he isn't one to tell a tale about something like that. About other things, maybe, but he wouldn't waste my time if he hadn't really hit that bear."

"Then Stan saw the bear. He wouldn't waste your time either. And I definitely heard it in the woods. Not that I ever heard a wounded bear before. But it sounded like one, falling and lumbering along leadenly and twigs on the ground snapping and birds hysterically scattering and all that."

"Then the bear's somewhere in there and feeling pretty sick, if he had to fake being dead. Or could be he was nearly dead when you saw him and that lying down was real and by now he's died. I'm going to look for him. For the time being you people stay indoors. If you'll let me, I'll phone my wife from your house and tell her where I am. Then if any important calls come for the game warden on your number, yell into the woods after me. Sound around here travels far."

He calls from our phone and goes into the woods. We shut the downstairs windows and doors. We have lunch, I read and stare out the window, Susan returns to her translation work. The game warden knocks on the front door an hour later.

"Didn't see even a hint of him," he says. "I think you'll have to live with the thought of an injured cub on the peninsula for a little while, though I doubt he'll be back your way. He'll probably keep moving till he reaches the point. That's where I'm going to wait for him for the day. If I don't find him and nobody else sights him, I'll have to assume he died along the way."

"Any chance of there being bigger bears around?" I say.

"If there was, you would have seen her protecting her cub. That guy's all by himself and lost for sure."

He drives off in his van. Susan and I sit on the porch steps looking at the woods.

"Poor little baby bear," she says.

"One car every fifteen minutes on that road and he has to pick that time to try to cross it."

"Maybe he crossed it lots of times, looking or sniffing for his way back home."

"You know, I'm not sure if this is the right time to tell you, but the game warden was only fibbing about there being a bear hit by a car. After he came here, when you were doing something else for a minute, I asked him to go along with the story about it being lost and so forth."

"Oh, don't be a fool."

"Yes, of course."

She goes inside and back to her work. I continue my reading. I finish the novel and start another. It's also entertaining but not very good. I cook dinner and we eat and read and watch part of a movie on television and light a fire and have ice cream topped with fresh fruit and then go to bed.

"Good night, sweetie," she says, turning off her light.

"Remember what we said we might resume doing once the game warden went?" I say.

"I'm tired and don't feel like it."

"All right."

I call the game warden two days later and he says the bear was never seen again. There's also an article about it in the state's largest daily newspaper on the page dealing with our county's news. Our names are in it and the game warden's and the man who hit the bear with his car. The article seems to be accurate till it comes to the part where we first came across the bear in the woods. It says I slashed at it with my axe while Susan threw stones at it, and though we missed it each time, we did manage to scare it away.

THE BARBECUE

I'm at this apartment with several people who came over for a backyard barbecue at nine o'clock but hadn't known because the hosts couldn't get ahold of everyone that the barbecue had been postponed, when someone says "I've got to tell this story. All of you—no, everybody, you've got to listen to one of the wildest stories I've ever heard and which is all true. Every last word."

"The one with the dum-de-dum in the wall you told me yesterday when you got home?" a woman says.

"That one."

"Yes, tell it, they'll love it," she says from a chair in a circle of chairs and a couch we're all sitting in around this room, all of us drinking either the wine or beer we brought for the food we thought would be barbecued, and he says "All right, I'll tell it. Or maybe why don't you, Dee, as you can always tell stories way better than me."

"Not when I'm asked I can't. Besides, you were the one who first heard it and said you wanted to tell it so much, so just tell it, Ron."

"Come on, Ron," someone says, "one of you or the other. What happened with the dum-de-dum in the wall that was so wild?"

"Well down where I work, near the courthouses—"

"You a lawyer?"

"Yes and no. I'm a clerk to a federal judge. Anyway, near where I work, the district attorney also has his office."

"A federal district attorney?" I say.

"There is no federal district attorney. That's the U.S. attorney. From the Justice Department. They're down there too, but this district attorney I'm talking about is only for the city."

"Are you people going to let Ron tell his story," someone says, "or am I going to be forced to tell one of my own?"

"If you want, why don't you then," Ron says. "Maybe mine isn't that good after all."

"It's a great story," Dee says. "Will everybody please not interrupt Ron again and let him finish his story in one piece?"

"Okay. I promise no more questions," I say.

"Or interruptions."

"Or interruptions. Though I thought that was just about what I was saying with my no more questions."

"They're a bit different," someone says. "Because you don't have to interrupt a speaker with just a question. It could be with a scream. A belch. A boo. A—"

"I didn't mean literally. I meant—"

"I didn't mean literally either. When I said belch I thought—"

"Oh God," Dee says. "Ron, don't listen to them. Just continue speaking over their voices from where you left off."

"Where was that? It was so long ago I forgot."

"You were in the district attorney's office," someone says.

"I wasn't, my friend was. He works there. I clerk for a judge."

"What is it you do for the judge? Clerk? I mean, actually file things, or do you help with the legal work?"

"To be a law clerk you have to be a lawyer first," a woman says. "My brother was one. At least to have gone through law school and come out with one of the top grades."

"That's right," Ron says. "Most of them are right out of law school, but I'm not. Dee, could you reach me another beer? There's a six-pack right behind you on the floor."

"I'll get you one cold from the kitchen," one of the hosts says.

"No, this one's fine. We had it on ice before we got here. Anybody else want one?"

"Dammit, I'm really sorry about the barbecue. We tried. Next time I'm getting everyone's last name or phone number just in case. Maybe we can scrape something together in the kitchen or just send out."

"I don't know about the rest of them," Ron says, "but I welcome no food for a change." He pops open the beer and drinks from the can. The music on the tape deck ends and one of the hosts goes through his tapes. "You have Herbie Hancock?" someone says. "Coltrane?" We talk about a lot of different things. Politics, books, the garbage strike, mostly movies. Then Dee says "You know what?" and a few people say "What?" and she says "My husband never did get to tell his story about that unbelievable wall thing that happened downtown."

"It was only partly downtown, but mostly up," Ron says.

"Now would be a good time to tell it," I say. "At least I'm interested to hear."

"Tell it," someone says.

"I left off at the DA's office?"

"Just start from the beginning," Dee says.

"All right. Down near where I work at the Federal Building, I always meet a friend of mine in the district attorney's office for lunch. Or almost, when we meet. We went to law school together and before that knew each other for summers on Lake Michigan. So he tells this true story which is what I'm going to tell you. What happened is that the district attorney's office gets lots of crazy phone calls. Maybe ten to twenty a day, like a police station. But one it got a couple weeks ago was from a woman who says there's a man in the next apartment who's invading her with X rays."

"She didn't say bombarding?" Dee says.

"Bombarding might be the right scientific word, but what Jack said she said was 'I'm being invaded by X rays by the man next door.' " Everyone laughs.

"No, wait, it goes on. Jack says to her 'Don't worry, lady, everything will be all right. It takes years and years for human bones to accumulate any degree of roentgen poisoning from the X rays' gamma rays,' not really knowing what he was saying medically but hoping she'd take it as sound knowledge and go away and she does for that day. But next day and the two days after that, she calls the district attorney's office and says the man next door's still invading her with X rays and this time much worse than before. She's getting sick, nervous and dizzy and doesn't know what to do to stop him. Well, a few people in the office had a quick discussion and decided she'd be calling every day if they didn't come up with something. So Jack, who took the last call, says to her 'Why don't you line your wall with aluminum foil? X rays can't penetrate metal, right? You do that and though he might aim his X rays straight at you and all month if he wants, the foil will foil and repel it.' He only said repel. I shouldn't try to make the story any more than it is, as it doesn't need it. But now she tells Jack that the man's been invading her through all her walls for the last day—as being sort of a railroad flat apartment they live in, all their rooms are perfectly aligned, bathroom with bathroom, kitchen, kitchen, and so on. So Jack says 'Then cover all your walls that border the man's apartment with aluminum foil and there won't be a chance you'll be invaded with X rays unless he does it through your windows or door. Can he do that?' he asks and she says not through the windows and the door has a burglar-proof iron shield. So she tells him she'll try what he advised her and sure enough she calls back a few days later and says she lined the walls on one entire side of her apartment with aluminum foil and now she isn't being invaded anymore by X rays. All the dizziness, nausea and the little craziness she got from the rays are gone now, she says, and she thanks him and hangs up."

"That's just fantastic," someone says.

"It's not even half the story," Dee says. "Not even a quarter."

"You see, all's normal on the phone at the district attorney's office for a few days," Ron says. "Just the typical ten-to-twenty crank to crackpot calls per day from other people, when the woman calls again and wants to speak to Jack. He gets on and says 'What's wrong now? X rays getting through the aluminum foil?' 'Oh no,' she says, 'haven't had any trouble from rays since I put the foil up, but it's something just as bad in another way. Every day for the last three days a penis is being stuck through a wall into my apartment a few times, through the foil and all.' "

"A penis?" someone says, but Dee is shaking her head at Ron. "I'm sorry, honey, but you didn't tell it right. What I remember you saying how Jack said it was 'No, it's not the X rays I'm being invaded with now, but a penis through the wall.' "

"It's the same thing."

"Yeah, but it sounds better. Though you were right about before. It had to be an invasion and not a bombardment, with what I remembered just now about what she said about the penis. But finish your story."

"So Jack says 'A penis through your wall? Well, I don't think the aluminum foil's going to stop that, lady—absolutely no way.' But she says 'No, you don't understand. It's a real penis, like the X rays were. Every three hours or so in my non-sleeping hours it invades me through the wall. I only called you this time because you were so nice the last time and because when I called the police station about this, they either said they'd come over and never did or laughed at what I said.' Jack tells her she's right, it isn't a matter for the district attorney's office and that he'll phone her precinct station and have them send a man right away. He makes his call and the sergeant or someone says they don't have any records of any calls from the woman, but they'll check the complaint out. So a policeman goes over, Jack's later told, and there in her railroad flat in the South Bronx are five to six rooms with the same entire wall of each one of them stapled from floor to ceiling with aluminum foil. The policeman asks some questions and she says yes, a penis does come through the wall at a different place every time or at least not the same hole consecutively, but she hasn't seen one for half a day. He asks where she saw one last and she says 'Through that hole' and he says 'What hole?' because she's pointing to the aluminum foil and she says 'I cover it up every time it pops through and pulls back again because I'm even more afraid of the man invading me with X rays through that new hole.' The policeman gives her a card with his phone number on it and says if anything like a penis coming through the wall happens again, call him, and leaves the apartment. When he's walking down the stairs he hears her screaming 'Officer, come here, the penis is invading me through the wall again.' He runs back and there through this hole that wasn't there before is a penis stuck through the wall. He immediately knocks on the door of the next apartment and this old guy there answers and is arrested on the spot. A search later finds that the man has eight old dental office X ray machines which from time to time, as she said and which nobody was ever smart enough to thoroughly check out including my friend Jack, he used to stick through various holes in the wall separating their apartments and actually bombard her with lethal X rays."

"Come on," someone says. "It's a funny story, but it's not true."

"That's just it," Ron says, "it's all true. Jack swears by it. He was part of it."

"First of all, what apartment has that many holes in it?"

"You don't understand then," Dee says. "This is the South Bronx. A tenement. The worst kind of building in the worst American slum."

"Why does everyone always pick on the poor South Bronx to suspend our disbelief? People get holes in their walls everywhere and when they do they usually get them patched up."

"In the South Bronx, or in the worst parts of it we'll say, you can't get them patched up so easily. Hardly any supers. Just absentee landlords living in Queens. And no carpenter or maintenance person will drive to within a mile of the place."

"Then if you can't get the local wino or kid from downstairs to patch up the holes, you do it yourself. You get a little plaster of paris and water and a mixing stick—"

"She's an old lady."

"Ron didn't say anything about her being old."

"She was old, believe me," Ron says. "Just by the way Jack described her with his voice and what she said, she was old."

"Okay, she's old, but so old she can't smear a little Spackle from a can?"

"Wait a minute. Why are you making this into such a big deal? It's just a story I heard."

"But you're telling me it's a true story. So I'm telling you that even in true stories old people use prepared Spackle to patch up holes."

"Maybe she can't afford prepared Spackle or even know it exists," Dee says. "Some people don't. And I don't think the woman, the way Ron spoke about her, was that educated or let's say sophisticated about modern plastering techniques or in that neighborhood wanted to walk outside that much if a hardware store was still around. Half the buildings and stores there have been deliberately burned down in the last few years. And most of those fires started soon after the tenant or merchant left his apartment or store."

"You saying people who aren't arsonists no longer go outside in the South Bronx?"

"I'm saying that where this woman lives hardware stores might be few and far between."

"Let's change the subject," someone says.

"Fine, but let me finish with Ron and Dee. She has holes in her wall, your woman. Many of them and on every wall adjoining the man's apartment, okay? But even with the foil over them, how come the policeman didn't look through at least one of those holes she said the penis and X rays came through? To me that's unheard of."

"Maybe he sensed she didn't want him tearing her foil apart," Ron says. "Or he came to her place very skeptical of her story to begin with, but I don't exactly know. But I'll tell you, even with some of the federal cases we get before us, you can't believe how many of the so-called thorough investigations the government's supposed to have completed against the accused are just plain half-assed."

"And the police station with no record of her calls?"

"She could've been phoning the wrong precinct all the time."

"Then wouldn't they have given her the right precinct to call once they learned her address? I don't know. I can't buy it except as a made-up story, though I'll shut up now."

"It really all happened," Dee says, "though maybe some parts of it are a little changed in passing from Jack to Ron to us. But you haven't heard the punch line yet."

"You mean there's more?" I say.

"They book the guy for trespassing," Ron says. "And not for the X ray machines either, since they only had the woman's word that they penetrated the wall."

"Why not for invasion of property?" someone says. "Or indecent exposure? That's what they should have got him for," when the doorbell rings.

"Oh no," one of the hosts says, "not more guests we can't feed. You get it this time, Lillian," he tells his girlfriend. "I can't face it."

Three people come in with six-packs of beer and what's left of their gallon of wine. They tell everyone they just came from a soccer match at Randall's Island where the new much-publicized Brazilian soccer player did these incredible things with the ball like bounce it all the way downfield on his head and another time keep it spinning on his toes a half a minute before he casually dropped it in for a goal, and now they're starving. "They doubled the food prices there since they paid three million for the King."

The host says "I'll get you something—we've got to have some food in there for them to eat, Lillian," and someone says "No no, don't bother," but they go into the kitchen and come out with a platter of peanut butter and jelly sandwiches on white bread. I refuse one. He says "Go on. I bet you haven't had one since you last loved them as a kid," and I take one and bite into it and don't like the taste and texture at all. "Maybe if it was on dark bread it'd be more palatable," I say, "but thanks." I open another beer. Lillian tells the three new people about the story Ron told that had everyone splitting their sides and which had to be the wildest thing she ever heard.

"You think you can tell it again?" she says and Ron says "I've told that story one too many times already. You tell it, Dee."

"I can't tell stories well except to my classes and you. I always get the facts straight but the sequence of events mixed up."

"I'll tell it," I say. "A shorter version, if I can even remember that much." I start the story and am corrected and interrupted a couple dozen times along the way. I end with the trespassing punch line, which in my retelling of it I call "the moral of the story," and again everyone laughs throughout the story and cracks up hardest at the end of it, including the doubter from before and Ron and Dee.

NOT CHARLES

So we have a son. I mean give birth to one. Liz does. I'm pacing the hospital waiting room for a while when a nurse comes in and says "Douglas Watson?" and I say no and she goes over to the man who'd only been in the room a couple of minutes and stood up when she said Douglas Watson to me and says "You're Mr. Watson then."

"Yes, what's wrong?" and she says "You've had a son, Mr. Watson, and both mother and child are doing well." Then she comes over to me and says "You're. . .?" and looks at her clipboard and I say "Douglas Mineger."

"That's why I got confused. A few hours ago when you said who you were and the other Mr. Watson, I mean, Douglas, wasn't here yet—well, I must've now thought you were him. Two Douglases in the same waiting room having sons. That's something that's never happened to me before, not even two Douglases having any kind of babies the same day I think."

"I had a son?" and she says "Didn't I just tell you?"

"You told him, not me, except for what you said now. That's terrific. How are they? My wife. Lizabeth and the child. Charles. Just yesterday we decided. How's Charles? Good God, that's the first time I'm saying his name when he's actually out and alive."

"Both are doing fine now. A minor respiratory complication did develop with your boy, but nothing to worry about."

"His breathing? He wasn't breathing and you slapped him and he began breathing?"

"Little more complicated than that, but he's all right. The doctor will be here soon to explain." She checks the clipboard. "Well, you both don't have the same doctor at least. That would have been too strange. If you did and your wives' names were the same and even your family ones, let's say, besides your own first names, well I'm sure you'd be taking home each other's baby, not that it would make much difference by then. But good luck to you both, and your doctor will be here to see you soon also, Mr. Watson," and she goes.

"Excuse me," I say to her. But she's out of the room and flying down a corridor. I run after her. "Nurse? Miss?" She's through some swinging doors marked *authorized personnel only*. I catch up and tap her shoulder.

"Mr. Watson, what is it?"

"Mineger. I want to ask you—"

"The names. Of course. Both—"

"My son. I'm still not clear. What's actually wrong? More than the breathing, or because of it. Will he be damaged from now on in any way? Will he even live? I started to ask you in the waiting room but you ran away."

"You did? I'm sure I didn't hear. Yes, he'll live. Or about as good a chance as any new baby has, with or without minor birth problems, which in the first day or so we can never be absolutely sure of. So I can't answer you positively a hundred percent. His condition's serious but stable. That's what it says here. But I'll tell you, that's, as I said, what you can say for almost any new baby. Only your doctor can really tell you what's wrong. For that, you'll have to wait. And only reason I'm hurrying like this is because I'm already due on another delivery, so you'll have to excuse me now." She goes.

"How long will the doctor be?" I yell.

She puts her finger over her lips, goes through another set of doors. I must be in some ward. Not a ward. Individual rooms on both sides of the corridor with sick-looking people on the beds inside them. Not the maternity wing. Mostly old people, some fairly young. My age. No babies, no kids. Bandages around their heads, some of them. Some of them their chests, arms and legs, one with one leg. Special place. Dying place? Also different medicinal smells.

A doctor or orderly, an orderly, wheeling an empty litter out of a patient's room and now towards me and into another patient's room, stops and says "Can I ask what you're doing here? Visiting hours aren't till six."

"I'm from maternity. My wife. I wanted to ask a nurse who came through here, just went out there—"

"Nobody's allowed in this area anytime without a pass. You want to wait for your nurse back there?"

"Sure. Sorry. I know I don't belong here. But you see, the nurse,

Miss Linko or Linkon I think the little thing on her chest said, walked through these doors when she and I were talking before, as I wanted to know what was wrong, if anything was—"

He's pointing to the doors. I go past them. The other Douglas is talking to a doctor, they shake hands and go different ways. I go to my wife's room. She's not there. I sit in the waiting room and wait. A half-hour passes. A nurse passes carrying a pile of those absorbent bed pads, and with some hospital form between her lips. "Excuse me, I know you're busy, but you think it'd be possible to see Dr. Boyce now, or my wife?"

"She's patient? Staff?"

"Patient. Three-ten. Lizabeth Dillard. She goes by her maiden name. I'm Douglas Mineger. I didn't mean to stop you. That looks heavy. Can I carry it for you? Well, we had a baby boy about an hour ago or less, though she's not back in her room yet."

"Just sec. Rid this." She delivers the pads, walks past me with her hand up to tell me she'll be back in a moment, comes back. "Miss Dillard's still in recovery and Dr. Boyce is in the delivery room."

"When he's through I'd like to see him, please. It's important. And if my wife gets back to her room without my knowing it, that too?"

"He'll get to you in time."

I wait. I fall asleep and dream of a baby being stabbed. Actually, it's a doll, it turns out, and then the doll's thrown out of our apartment window by that orderly from before, though I didn't see who stabbed it. Just a hand with a white sleeve and wristwatch. I know what the dream means. I wake up in a sweat. Not the watch though, that's too open to interpretation. Maybe I need something to eat, and coffee. But if I go downstairs to the cafeteria I won't be here if Dr. Boyce comes. Or when Liz gets out of recovery. I go to her room. Not there. To the newborn baby room at the end of another hall. Several shades cover the windows. I can't even peek underneath but do hear lots of crying and whines. To the nurses' station. "Any news about my baby boy? Mineger and Lizabeth Dillard's? Or news about my wife Ms. Dillard?"

"Room and bed number?"

"Three-ten. C."

She goes through a batch of records, pulls Liz's up. "Has Dr. Boyce seen you?"

"Nobody's seen me. I was sleeping, maybe that's why."

"Sleeping in the waiting room or your wife's?"

"The room there."

"Then he would have looked in and nudged you if he'd seen you sleeping. I'll page him. He's through with his other delivery. Your wife's still in recovery."

"Isn't that a long time to recover from a delivery? I don't know, but it seems so if it wasn't a Caesarean."

"It wasn't. And it's not that unusual."

"And the baby? Where is he? With my wife? In that newborn baby room at the end of the hall—the nursery?"

"Neither. I think Dr. Boyce wants to speak to you."

"Listen, what's wrong? What is it?"

"Please hold it a minute? Paging Dr. Boyce. Dr. Boyce. To third floor station." I hear this over the P.A. system maybe a second after each word I see her speaking into the microphone. "Dr. Boyce. Boyce. Third floor station. Call or come in." She flicks off the switch. "You don't look well. Maybe you'd like to rest. Water?"

"Sure I don't look well. I'm worried about my wife and son. Nurse Linko, I think her name is, mentioned his breathing. At first I thought it was something very minor. Slap on the back, like that, but now this."

"You mean Miss Lunkowitz?"

"Lunkowitz, Lunkowitz. And this Dr. Boyce on the mike just before has to see me so much? Look, it took us six years of trying to have this child. We could've adopted one. We were thinking of it. Then she got pregnant. Long after the great experts said we couldn't. They didn't know. Or else our natures changed. I don't know about such things. But this might be the only time she can get pregnant."

"Just calm down. Everything'll be all right."

"All right, I'm calm. I'll be calm. Because I know some people might not think that's very important, our having a child. Believe me, we heard it all. Lots of kids need to be adopted. All kinds of kids. Girls, boys. Kids in other countries. Good kids here, but mistreated, abandoned, etcetera. But we wanted one of our own, then we'd see about adopting another. But we wanted the first one to be the one we couldn't think we could give back. Can you understand? I'm saying if we lose this baby my wife will be very upset. Very—much more than me, though I'll be very sad and upset too. So I want to know what's happening now so I can be preparing for my wife for it if she suddenly comes down now."

"I think you better sit down. I don't know anything, Mr. Mineker. Honestly."

"Then where's my son?"

"It says here in a special incubator."

"Says where? What is that thing?"

"Just a patient's file. I can't show it to you."

"Then the special incubator. What's it for?"

"Dr. Boyce will tell you."

"Then where's that incubator and where's Dr. Boyce?"

"Wherever it is, you won't be able to see it till Dr. Boyce says you can. I've paged him. If he can't come, he knows where to call in."

"That was that third floor station over the P.A.?"

"That's us right here, yes."

"How do you know he heard you?"

"Because he hasn't left."

"But how do you know?"

"We know. He checks out. If he did, I'd be the second or third person to learn of it and within minutes after he left. He also would have passed this way, probably. Or phoned this station. He's heard, in other words. If he was in the men's room or private dining area, he heard. And if he's been in some completely out-of-the-way intercom place like an operating room, then someone would tell him. That's what they do. Either personally by mouth or over his pocket page. Or one of his staff will tell me where he is if he can't be reached by hospital intercom and his page is on the blink. But it's not. And he's not in any operating theater or room, because by now in just the time we've been speaking here, I would have known."

"Please page him again."

"You hear all those pages? There's room for only so many and too many to the same person for the same reason is considered excessive and also tends to confuse."

I didn't hear much before. Now I do. Paging this doctor, that nurse. So-and-so to room 607, piece of equipment to corridor D. Numbers, names. Letters, codes. All the time it seems to be going. But if I was able to block it out before, why can't Dr. Boyce? Probably because he's trained himself not to. Maybe, maybe not.

"Please page him again. Also try to get him on his private page?"

"Okay, but sit down. I'll get you some water. Paging Dr. Boyce. Boyce. To third floor station. Q-E." She dials a telephone, says "Lily? Dora. Can you get the doctor to nursing third floor? Much. Thanks."

I sit. She gets me water. I drink. I'm still thirsty and I hold up my cup. She says coming right up. "Not necessary," I say, standing. "Because what am I doing? I'm a big boy."

"Just sit."

The doctor comes. "Mr. Mineker."

He tells me about my son. Something about some president's last son who was born with and died from the same disease.

"I don't understand."

Membrane over the lungs. Often fatal. Condition's critical. Oh yes, now I remember. Tragic, tragic story, he says. And I can see him now. Downstairs we go. My wife know? He told her a few minutes ago. Took it like a trooper. Some mothers he's told have gone totally out of control. To the subbasement, then up a short flight. Boy's there. Face upwards in this transparent incubating thing. A rounded plastic coffin, looks more like, once they unhook the tubes and seal up the tube holes. Fighting for his life. Hup two. In out, out in. "Breathe," I say, "breathe, breathe." Small room. Like a bunker or interior of a submarine. No windows or slits. Gray cinderblock walls. Dials, pipes. Another baby's there, also in one of these spaceage things. Not looking any different than the incubators I saw this morning in the nursery on Liz's floor. Trying to keep these babies out of sight? Too sad to see for any new parent and maybe they're contagious. But he looks good. Other baby doesn't. Healthy-looking hairy ox our son is, though I don't know what he weighs. "He'll make it," I say.

"We certainly hope so."

"What are his chances?"

"Nurse," he says and asks about the readings and parameters or something.

They talk. Point decimal point signal percentage degree.

"We'll know more in a few hours, maybe not for a day," he says. "We better go. This is intensive care and the nurses get awfully feisty if we're here too long just to look and we don't even have masks on, though they understand."

We go upstairs. He walks me to the door of my wife's room, tells me he'll get back to us in a while and even quicker if there's any major change, yells "Hold it" to the elevator car that just opened and runs to it as I go into her room.

We kiss and I sit by her bed.

"Boyce know any more what the chances are?" she says.

"Probably no more than he told you. Hours. Maybe a day, even two."

"What luck. Damn, why us?"

"Why anybody?"

"Forget anybody. Why him? Why us? Tell me."

"What do you want me to say? Anyway, how do you feel?"

"Feel? Oh Douglas." She holds out her arms.

"I feel lousy too."

"Douglas, hold me. I need you too," still holding out her arms.

"Of course. I'm sorry." I hold her hands.

"Oh Christ, thanks a lot."

"I'm sorry, I'm sorry. But I was so into my own misery, I forgot yours. I was thinking about Charles down there."

"Charles? Who's that? He doesn't have a name yet."

"I thought we decided."

"If he dies we have to give him a name? My father's? Two Charleses I have to bury in one year?"

"Hey wait a minute, bad stuff you're talking. We have to believe he's going to live."

"Okay, I'm believing, but why don't I absolutely feel it?"

"Because you didn't see him. I did. He's strong. Breathing well. He's beautiful. Hair on his head already and these big cheeks. He even looks like you."

"Go on, don't say it. Like me? How?"

"The face. I told you. Big cheeks and being so beautiful. And almost the same physique as you. Comparatively, I mean. I bet he weighs more than eight pounds."

"Eight-three. But he's not just fat? He's tall?"

"He's built perfectly for his age. He'll make it."

"Oh Doug, if he doesn't what are we going to do? I'm so sad."

"So am I." I hold her.

"That feels better. Doug, I want to see him."

"I don't think you can get out of bed yet."

"Of course I can. I've already been out of bed."

"I thought you weren't supposed to for a few days."

"It was a local. Sooner the better they said."

"It'll be too emotional for you."

"No, I have to." She rings for the nurse. The nurse comes. "I want to see my baby, please."

"I think you should wait a few more hours before you can be moved."

"That's what I told her."

"I heard sooner the better I should be walking around and I've already gone to the bathroom myself."

"You shouldn't have," the nurse says. "You had a rough delivery."

"What rough? They gave me an injection. I delivered a baby. Now I feel good. You don't want me to walk, wheel me there."

"Let me speak to Dr. Boyce."

"No doctor. Nothing. I want to see my baby to tell him how he mustn't die."

"I'm sure Dr. Boyce never said anything about your son going to die."

"He might die. It's possible. And why do you think a doctor should know everything more about my baby than I? He was in me for the maximum period. I still feel him inside. He must still feel himself inside me. He just misses me, that's what it is. I'm not suddenly dreaming this but really feeling it—he just misses me somehow and wants some word from me, a look or little whisper from me, a communication or encouragement of some sort if just through the space and incubator between us that he's going to be okay and I'm not in there with him not because I don't want to and his breathing problem is just a simple problem that can be worked out if he does what I say and breathes harder and clearer and works with the machine better to keep more of the problems away."

"Just stay here," the nurse says. "I'll get the resident."

"Hell with the resident. Douglas, will you look for a wheelchair?"

"I think we should wait till the nurse speaks to the doctor."

"Douglas, didn't you hear what I just said I was feeling? I have to see him downstairs. If they stall us till I get a doctor it could be too late. Now find me a chair."

"Please get her a chair," I say to the nurse.

"They have to be called down for and sent up."

"I saw one outside the next room."

"Then it must belong to one of the patients there."

"Borrow it, Douglas."

"I'm going to do that."

"I'm not a policeman," the nurse says.

The door of the next room is slightly ajar. I tap on it. I knock.

"Yes?" a woman says.

"Excuse me," I say through the door, "but if you don't mind I'd like to borrow the wheelchair out here for a few minutes."

"Who are you?"

"The husband of a woman next door who just had a baby. Well, our baby's very sick and we want to go downstairs to see it."

"The baby who was born or an older child of yours?"

"Just take the chair, Doug," Liz yells from her room.

"Baby who was born. Please, we're in a rush. A boy. Something about a membrane, lung disease. The president's son disease it's called, or syndrome—I forget. But it's very serious."

"I know which disease you mean. Sure, borrow it. It's the hospital's. If you don't bring it back I'll get another. And best of luck."

I wheel the folded-up chair into Liz's room. I can't get it apart. The nurse isn't there.

"Pull it by the bars on the side," Liz says.

"No," the other patient in the room says. "The arms on top—the arm rests—out while you're pulling them a little up."

I do as she says. Wheelchair unfolds and I help Liz into it. Dr. Boyce comes into the room with the nurse while I'm wheeling Liz out.

"Where you going?" he says.

"To help our son," Liz says. "I have to, so don't try to stop us."

"Will you get back in bed, Liz? Now please." His face looks bad. He and the nurse help Liz into bed. She's already crying. He covers her up to her chest and strokes her hair. Points to the one chair for me and sits opposite us in the wheelchair. The nurse stands behind him. He tells us our son has died. We break down and cry. The patient across the room is crying. The doctor and nurse look sad too. "We did everything we could," he says. Lots of other things he says. He squeezes my hand, Liz's hand, pats my shoulder, starts to go.

"By the way," he says at the door. "I know this is the wrong time to mention this—it always is—but time is so essential in this matter that I'm forced to ask you. Would it be against your principles or religious faith to allow an autopsy done on your son and then to give him to science? It would be very helpful to us."

"Can we think about it?" I say.

"We don't need any time," Liz says. "My one and only child? For so long we tried to have him and now you want to cut him up and take every little piece of him away, even for important experiments? No. I'm sorry but we can't. He gets buried like my dad. Right beside him so every time I go see either of them, I can speak to them both."

"As you wish. Though maybe if your husband talked to you about it in the next few minutes—"

"He won't. I won't let him. The question's finished, all right?"

Liz is released the next day. For a couple of years after that we did everything the doctors said we should to conceive another child. Fertility pills. When that didn't work, birth control pills which she was suddenly taken off of and put on fertility pills. We risked having triplets, quintuplets, even worse. It all came to nothing. Sperm count low and my motility weak and her ova don't descend far enough to be fertilized and maybe even some other things, the doctors said. So we adopted a two-year-old girl from Vietnam who's now three. People have criticized us for that. Said we were playing politics with orphans. That in a tremendous drive to sway public opinion on behalf of its client nation, our country's president, with the assistance of several adoption agencies, and so on . . . pawns of war. Some people think we should try to find Giselle's real parents or relatives or at the very least send her back to a Vietnam adoption agency so she can grow up with a Vietnamese family or in a nice children's home. That she'll hate us for years to come if we don't send her back now. Even our own brothers and sisters have told us to do this. But we love her too much to give her up now. As far as the best thing for Giselle, who knows?

MY DEAR

Knock on the door.

"Come in."

Does, looks at me sitting at my desk, continues to look and I say "Yes, so, what do you want?"

Sits on the chair near me, folds her hands, looks to the left where the liquor cabinet is.

"It's a bit early, but would you like a drink?"

Unfolds her hands, looks at them, at her shoes and then at the floor around her shoes. I look there but don't see anything but her shoes and carpet they're on.

"What did you want to see me about?"

Looks straight at me.

"Me? No? So maybe you just wanted to come in here, not to see me about anything special, just to sit and talk awhile, that it?"

Still straight at me.

"Say something, will you, you can speak. Is it something about me, I've done, concerning you, or just something about you entirely unrelated to me? You feeling all right? Something else? Why were you looking so intently at the floor before?"

Just stares at me, never looks away.

"If you're not going to say anything, or even give me a sign with a different expression but that plain almost expressionless expression you have now, then why'd you bother even coming in here?"

Same expression.

"Then would you mind if I go back to my work?"

Same.

"I'm going back to my work, whether you mind or not, no offense meant, of course. It's just, well—you know. How can I—I mean, well—Dammit, you're making me inarticulate with your stares and expressionlessness. Uncomfortable too. Me, uncomfortable, because I don't like talking to myself or just about talking to myself when the person I'm supposedly talking with—but you know what I mean. I don't have to try and explain myself further."

"Yes you do."

"So. You do speak. I knew you did. I knew you didn't just suddenly lose your voice. If you had, I would have known about it sooner—permanently lost your voice, I mean. If you had only temporarily lost it—laryngitis, something like that—you would have told me, right? I mean, written it down. But that's silly. May I ask you a question?"

"Ask more than one. Ask two, ask four."

"One at a time. Why didn't you answer me before when I was asking you all those questions?"

"What questions?"

"Questions like why did you come into this room. In fact, why did you?"

Looks at the floor.

"Don't start again, please."

At the liquor cabinet.

"That again. The cabinet. I know you occasionally like a light drink—sherry, port, though never one so early, as I said. But is that it? Something happened that warrants an early drink?"

Ceiling.

"Please don't."

Still does.

"Okay, what do you see up there? Our neighbors on the third floor? Bird or a few through the next two ceilings and roof? Or maybe it's only our light fixture. That what you're staring at?"

Folds her hands together, wiggles her fingers, raises the fingers one by one till they're all raised though still interlocked.

"Making designs with your fingers?"

Shuts her eyes.

"Maybe you want to go to sleep."

Eyes open, look dreamy, slowly shut again and stay shut.

"I think you do want to go to sleep. You seem tired. If I'm right, and maybe that's what you came into this room to tell me, don't you think you'd be more comfortable in your own bed or stretched out on the living room couch rather than seated upright in this rather uncomfortable chair? I know, because I've sat countless times in that chair. It's very uncomfortable to sit in, I can just imagine what it'd be like to try and sleep in it. I don't even know why I bought it."

"You didn't."

"That's right. You gave it to me years ago. It was your father's. And you're speaking again. Nice to hear your voice again. And your eyes are open again. Nice to see them again too. But you don't know—"

"What don't I know?"

"No, I know you must know how distracting if not infuriating it is to speak to someone who doesn't answer you after that person first didn't answer back, then did and then goes into this speechless state of yours, pretending not to hear so looking at everything in the room but me."

"I did that?"

"You didn't?"

Floor.

"I hope you're not going to—"

Ceiling, liquor cabinet, hands, which she folds together, wiggles, unfolds, spreads out on her knees.

"Got another visual distraction—hands on your knees, huh?"

My shoes.

"Oh, still another one: my shoes."

My face.

"You already looked at my face without speaking—before, just after you came in. Excuse me, but what—"

She's looking at the window and whatever she sees through it in the street.

"I was saying: what's wrong with you? Why do you not talk, talk, not, etcetera? Why do you pretend I'm not speaking to you or that you can't hear me? Are you trying to get back at me for some reason, and if so, for what reason? You think I've all the time in the world to play these games with you, if they are games. I'm a serious person. Not always serious, but serious a lot of the time and don't like to be played with like this. A little, yes. That can be fun and if you only do it once a week or so and just for a few seconds to a minute, let's say, a welcome game. I can become too serious perhaps and need games and distractions like that. But when you do it one after the other and for so long a time: not speaking, speaking, etcetera, looking away, pretending I don't exist, do, etcetera, well it—well it what? You answer me. What do you think it does to me, even if I've already told you and am demonstrating now too."

Looks at the door.

"Good. The door. Very good idea. That is a door, my dear. The one you entered this room through and the one I'd like you to leave through very soon."

Turns around and looks at the back of the chair she's on.

"Then right now. I want you to leave right now. You're absolutely disturbing me from my work. Now stop looking at that chair. There's nothing important anywhere around or inside or under that chair, or certainly nothing as important to you as my work is to me. You're just staring at that chair to keep from speaking to me. You're intentionally disturbing and infuriating me, maybe even trying to drive me crazy, and I want it to stop. I want you to leave this room right now. I definitely want you to if you don't stop what you're doing and speak to me like a wife should to her husband who's speaking to her, if she wasn't provoked by him or something else into not wanting to speak to him, and that's normally. I want you to speak to me normally, just as I'd do to you if our situations were reversed."

Turns completely around, knees on the chair seat now and looks over the back of the chair to the floor.

"I said there's nothing behind or anywhere around that chair. I said—out. I've had enough, want you to get out."

I get up and go over to her. She stands on the chair, stares at the wall behind it.

"There's nothing there but an empty wall. Now come down and turn around and tell me why you're doing this to me. Have I ever done it to you? When you want to work, I let you. If you're working, I always, if I want to speak to you, knock on your door and say before I enter, 'Am I disturbing you?' If you say I am, I leave. If you say I am but should say what I want to, I do, but very quickly, and then leave. Even if you say to take my time saying what I want to say to you, I still say it quickly and leave. But I've never once, once—oh the hell with it," and pull her down to the chair, grab her shoulders and turn her around. She looks at me, opens her mouth.

"Well?" I say.

"Well what?"

" 'Well what'!"

"Yes, well what? What is it? What's wrong?"

"You're saying this, while staring me straight in the face, that you don't know?"

Pushes my hands off her shoulders, stands, leaves the room, slams my door shut.

"Good." I sit at my desk, go over my facts and figures again. I hear noises from her room. Slamming of doors, things thrown to the floor and against the walls.

"Forget it," I tell myself. "Concentrate on your work. You gave her every opportunity to explain herself, and what's more important than your work? She is, or of equal importance, each holding the top place in its own league, so to speak, but just have it out with her when she calms down: later in the day or tonight."

But the noises disturb me enough to keep me from my work, so I just sit listening to them. Then I get so mad at them that I get up, throw open the door and go down the hallway to her room. Her door's open, room's a mess. Broken things all over. Dresser and night tables turned over, clothes scattered around, some ripped. Plants broken, mirror smashed, things off their hinges, etcetera. She's packing a suitcase with her clothes. I knock on the door jamb. She continues packing. I go into the room.

"Where are you going?"

Continues packing.

"I said where are you going?" I say louder.

Slams the lid down and locks it, grabs the suitcase by its handle and starts for the door.

"Will you just answer me one more time? Where are you going or why are you going?"

"Which one of those two do you want me to answer? Oh, sorry, but I just answered you one last time as you asked me to," and leaves the room and heads for the front door further down the hall.

"Now that was a funny thing you just said," walking behind her. "Very funny indeed. But could you answer me two more times? Or really, these two particular questions I'm about to ask?"

Opens the door.

"Then just one question more?"

Leaves the apartment and starts downstairs to the ground floor.

"Then no questions. Don't answer any. Just go, see how much it bothers me, but take note of one last petition: never come back."

Stops on the bottom step, puts the suitcase down and looks up at me. "You want to know one last thing?"

"Yes. Finally. Yes."

"No, I shouldn't say it," and picks up the suitcase.

"Please say it. After all these years? One last thing? Give me that consideration. What?"

"You're not much fun, that's all. You are not much fun. And you want to know why?"

"One more last thing? This is my lucky day."

"You want to know why or not?"

"Yes. Please. I'm sorry for acting cynical. What?"

"No. I said I'd only say one last thing and here I've already said even more than that," and walks to the vestibule door.

"No, please tell me. Why aren't I much fun? Because I don't like to be repeatedly distracted and disturbed from my very important work? Because I don't like to be treated like a moron or a rug to step on or any such thing like that? Because I like to speak and behave normally with people—rationally, civilly, and especially with my wife? And expect the same from people, and especially from my wife, if I didn't do anything to make them or you behave irrationally or uncivilly or abnormally to me? Is that why? Tell me. Because I want or demand all that?"

Turns around and looks at me.

"Well?"

At the steps leading down from me. At the banister, newel, floor around the newel, walls on both sides of her, ceiling, then turns around and faces the lace curtain on the vestibule door, perhaps looks at the curtain and the vestibule and mailboxes if she can see them through the curtain.

"Well? You going to speak or not? You into your silent act again or not? If you only want to speak about why you're in and out of this silent act, then speak only about that, but what? What?"

Puts the suitcase down and leaves the building. I run after her. She's not on the street. I run to the park corner and look every possible way for her and then run to the avenue at the other end of the block and look for her there. She's nowhere around. I go back to the building. The vestibule door's locked. I ring several tenants' bells. One answers. "Yes?"

"It's Mr. Newman. I forgot my keys. Please let me in."

"How do I know it's Mr. Newman?"

"Does it sound like my voice?"

"On this cheap system, nothing sounds like any voice I know."

"Believe me, Mrs. Fried, it's me, Mr. Newman, second floor."

"What's your wife's name, quick?"

"Mora Spone. She doesn't use—she goes by her maiden name, and last December, if you remember, you came up for champagne to help us celebrate the start of our twelfth wedding anniversary."

She buzzes the vestibule door. I open it, pick up the suitcase and go upstairs. I didn't shut our front door. I go in our apartment. Maybe only my front door and apartment now. No, ours, Mora's here, lying on her bed. Raises her arms to me. Wants me to come to her. I do. Takes my hands, pulls me to the bed. I sit on it. Pulls me down to her and hugs me and rubs the back of my head and kisses my cheek and rests her lips on my ear. "I'm sorry," she says. "I lost control. I'm sorry. I hope it won't happen again."

THE WATCH

Man on the street says "Spare a quarter, sir?" I say "No, really, I haven't much myself." He says "That's all right. Thanks." I walk a few steps and think "What the hell, I had a pretty good day and can spare a little," and go back to the man and say "Sure, I can give you something," and put my hand in my pants pocket for a dime or quarter, but he looks so sad and sickly that I pull out the largest coin among all the change in my pocket and give it to him. It's my watch. I thought it was a half dollar. It felt like it, thin and round, but it's my pocketwatch. "Excuse me, I gave you that by mistake," and reach for my watch, but his hand closes on it.

"You gave me your watch. Thanks a lot," and sticks it in his pants pocket and starts walking away.

"It was a half dollar I wanted to give you."

"You wanted to give me the watch," and he keeps walking.

I run after him and grab him by the shoulder.

"Let go or I'll call a cop."

"I'll let go when you give back my watch. I didn't mean to give it and you know that. I was being absentminded, just pulled out the largest coin in my pocket because I was feeling extra generous, or what I thought was the largest coin, forgetting my watch was in that pocket too. Now give it back, please, or I'll have to make trouble for you."

"You don't take your hand off me, I'll make even bigger trouble for you."

I take my hand off him. "You don't understand. That watch was my father's. It's the only thing he left me. He got it from his uncle, who bought it somewhere overseas. It's the one valuable thing I own and my father owned. Now give it back. It has tremendous sentimental value to me."

"And to me it has money value."

"It has money value also, but I'd never sell it no matter how broke I was."

"I'm going to sell it because I'm broker than you ever were. Broker

65

than your father and mine both. Dead broke. Thanks for the handout," and he walks away.

"Police," I shout.

No policeman's around. It's night and on a busy downtown street and people are around and they stop just as they stopped when I was arguing with him at the corner before and now they listen and some ask among themselves what's happening but nobody asks me or the man or tries to step in.

"Listen, people," I say. "I gave that man my valuable old watch by mistake."

A few people laugh. The man's past the crowd by now. I run after him. People follow. I grab his arm. He's smaller than me and thinner, much thinner. He's all bone it seems. Dirty too. His coat smells. He has two coats and a jacket on I now see. His hair coming out from his cap looks like it hasn't been washed or combed for weeks. He has two sweaters on too. People have crowded around us again but several feet away. "People," I say, "please listen. Help me get my watch back. It's a long story. This man asked me for money for coffee—"

"I didn't say for coffee," the man says.

"He asked for money. 'Spare a quarter,' he said. I felt sorry for him and thought I was giving him a half dollar, but it was my watch by mistake."

"That's what I asked him," he says to them. "And that's what he gave, but not by mistake. Get your hand off me," he says to me.

"I will if you don't walk away."

"Okay. I won't."

I take my hand off him. He walks away. The crowd opens up so he can get through. I run to the man and grab him with both hands and say "I'm not letting you go again and I might even throw you to the ground and by mistake break your head if you walk away again."

"I won't then."

I let go of him and say to the crowd "Will someone please get a policeman to straighten this out?"

"There'll be one around soon," someone says. "There always are. What happened? You gave him your watch by mistake you say?"

"I thought it was a half dollar I was taking out of my pants pocket."

"How come you keep a watch in your pants pocket and not on your wrist?"

"It's a pocketwatch and I lost the chain on it a few years ago, so I keep it in my pants pocket instead. It's very old and valuable. I'd never just give it away. It's my only good possession, my only possession of any worth. I'm a poor jerk. I've a job that doesn't pay well at all."

"You think I make a lot of money?" the man says to the crowd. "I asked him for money. He gave me his watch. I thought that was really generous, but it's not the first time people gave me things valuable like that. Once a man gave me a hundred-dollar bill. He knew it was a hundred. He even said 'Here's a hundred, pal,' and that was more than twenty years ago. Ten years later a woman came up to me when she saw me with my hand out and gave me a brooch. She knew it was a brooch. She unpinned it right from her jacket lapel and handed it to me without a word and walked away. I thought it was glass but I got two hundred for it. I bet it was worth a thousand then. People have done that over the years. A new radio here, a twenty-dollar bill there. So now, ten years after that lady, this guy gives me a valuable watch. I believed that he gave it to me because he wanted to and I still believe that. Only he, unlike the man with the hundred and the brooch lady, went back on his giving me it. But that's too bad for him. Once you give, you can't take it back. You make a mistake like that, you have to pay for it."

"He has a point," a man says.

"Only if he's telling the truth," a woman says, "which he isn't."

"How do we know?"

"You saying you believe a pig like that?"

"Pig though he may be, and I don't think it's for us to judge just because our clothes and appearances are better, he could still have a point. The watch-giver might have changed his mind. Should the beggar be penalized for that?"

"Yes, people have a right to change their minds."

"Not where I come from," the beggar says.

"They do have that right in most cases," I say, "not that that has anything to do with the situation here. I never intended giving him the watch. But if you people are only going to talk and talk about it, I'm going to get my watch back in my own way."

I try to get my hands in the pants pocket where he put the watch. He pushes my hand away and I grab one of his arms and start twisting it behind his back.

"Leave him alone," a man says. "He's so frail you'll kill him."

"But I have to do something," I say, letting him go. "That watch is worth over five hundred dollars."

"It is?" the beggar says. "Then I bet I'll be able to get a hundred for it."

"Why don't you just give him a hundred for it," someone says to me, "and be done with it. You pay for your mistakes like that man said."

"I don't have a hundred. Who carries a hundred on him these days? Maybe plenty do, but I only have a twenty on me, maybe less."

"I won't take twenty when I can get a hundred," the beggar says.

"What's this all about?" a policeman says.

I explain my story. The beggar explains his. The crowd stays around us. The policeman says to the beggar "Why don't you take the twenty and let the guy off light? You see the sentimental attachment it has for him."

"I'm starting to get sentimentally attached to it too," the beggar says.

"Twenty-five," I say, counting the money in my wallet. "That's all I have besides my fare home." I hold the money out to him. "I shouldn't even be giving you this, but I just want it back without any more fuss."

"Take it," the policeman says to the beggar.

"Take it," a few people say.

"I think he should hold out for fifty," a man says.

"Mind your business," the policeman says.

"Fifty I'll hold out for then," the beggar says.

"I don't have fifty," I say. "I have twenty-five and change when I didn't even think I had that."

"Someone here you know who can loan you another twenty or twenty-five?" the policeman says.

"Why should they? What I'm offering's more than fair. And I don't know anyone around here. It's not my neighborhood. I went to that movie theater there, because it's cheap, but I live uptown."

"Then I don't know what to say. Take the twenty-five," he says to the beggar. "I've work to do. This man wants his watch back and to get home."

"Take it," some people say.

"I still think he should hold out for fifty," that man says again.

"Keep quiet about what you think," the policeman says.

"I know my rights. I can open my mouth when I want to except when it's to yell fire in a theater when I know there isn't one."

"But you're making it worse for the watch-owner."

"What do I care for him?"

"No, I decided," the beggar says. "I can't give it away for just twenty-five."

"Then I'll have to take the watch and the two of you to the station so this man can file a complaint against you for his watch, and you, if you want, against him for breach of giving you it, or whatever that's called."

"Okay by me," the beggar says. "I've nothing much doing tonight and that watch is worth it."

"Nothing I can do about it," I say, "and at least the watch will be safe."

"The watch," the policeman says, holding out his hand.

The beggar puts his hand in the pocket the watch is in. Puts his other hand in his other pants side pocket. Feels through all the pants pockets and then all the pockets in his jacket and shirt and one of the sweaters with pockets on it and his coats. "I can't find it," he says. "I don't know what happened."

"Oh no," I say.

"You have holes in your pockets?" the policeman says to him.

"Sure I have holes. But I didn't think in the pocket where I put the watch. That one I had change in. So I also lost all my change." He feels in that pocket again. "Yeah, I have a hole in it. Must have been coming on for a long time and then all of a sudden tore apart."

"Oh no, oh no," I say. "My watch," and I run back to the place where I first met the beggar, looking at the sidewalk along the way. No watch. I go back to the beggar and the crowd and walk all around them and then walk back to the place where I first met him, looking at the sidewalk along the way. No watch. Some people from the crowd follow me the second time. The beggar and policeman follow them. Everyone seems to be looking with me including the beggar. "If anyone finds a watch," I yell, "tell me. Please tell me. A pocketwatch. No fob chain. A silver watch, roman numerals on the face, no inscription or design on the back and it's all by itself, not in a case."

"If I find," someone says.

I don't find the watch. Nobody does, or if they do, they don't say anything. "Please search him," I say to the policeman. "He might be lying."

"I'm not lying," the beggar says. "I have holes." He pulls his pants pockets out. He has holes in them. Then the side pockets of his outer coat. Holes.

"Please search him," I say. "He might be hiding the watch. He could have dropped it through the hole in his pocket to some place deeper inside the coat."

"I didn't," the beggar says.

"Do you mind a search?" the policeman says to him.

"Yes, I mind."

"If he minds, I can't search him. I can take him to the station and you can press charges there just as he can press them against you later for having him brought there if your charges turn out to be untrue, but I can't search him here just on your word. I can there, but he does seem to have holes in all his pockets."

"Let the cop search you," someone in the crowd says. "That way they'll know you've nothing to hide."

"Look, I'll give you ten dollars to let the policeman search you," I say to the beggar. "If the watch isn't on you I'll know it was really lost and then I can maybe do something about getting it back."

"Ten dollars? I lost everything else tonight, so what do I have to lose? Okay."

I give him a ten.

The policeman searches him. "No watch," he says, "unless he has a hiding place in all the clothes he has on that I can't find."

"Find it then," I say.

"I searched him. He doesn't seem to have anything on him but clothes."

"Now you're a watch and ten dollars out," someone says to me. "Try for more. Give the bum another ten for nothing and then your last five."

"That's all right," I say. "After the watch, nothing hurts."

"Excuse me," the policeman says to me. "Unless you want to press charges against this man, though I can't see what you'd gain by it, I'll have to go."

"What about me?" the beggar says. "How come you don't ask me the same thing about him?"

"All right," the policeman says to him. "Do you want to press charges?"

"No. I was only saying. As if you thought I didn't have something to complain about too."

"Sure," I say to the policeman. "Go. I'll continue to look for it. And honestly, thanks a lot."

I look at the sidewalk around me. The policeman goes. Most of the crowd goes. I walk to the place where I last grabbed the beggar and then back to the street corner again. The beggar's still there and says "If it's all right with you I'd like to help you look for your watch. I really don't have it on me. Not hidden. Nothing. If I did I'd be gone by now, wouldn't I?"

"Unless you want to prove something to me or yourself that I'm unaware of, then I guess so."

"I swear I don't want to prove anything."

"Why not then? Four eyes are better, but you have to understand that I'm not paying you to look, though I will give you another ten if you find it."

We search together and in different places for more than half an hour. During that time the beggar tells me his name and I tell him mine. Several people come up and ask us what we're looking for. Either Tom or I or both of us tell them. A few of these people join in the search for a while. We don't find the watch. Finally I say to Tom "It's not here. Someone must have picked it up or I don't know what. Maybe I'll put a notice in the paper for it. I'm going though."

"I'll look around a while longer. If I find it where can I get hold of you?"

"You won't find it." I leave.

I hear someone running up behind me a minute later. "Say Gene," Tom says. He's holding out a ten. "I didn't think it's fair to keep this. I should have let myself be searched for nothing. You were right. I shouldn't have kept the watch in the first place. If I had to for a few minutes, then I shouldn't have put it in my pocket. I knew I had holes in most of my pockets. No reason why I wouldn't have gotten holes in the rest of them or at least one more of them. I'm sorry for causing you so much trouble, because if anybody knows how you feel, it's me. My dad once gave me his gold cigarette case and I had to hock it when I needed money. I waited too long and when I went to get it back it was already sold and I still feel that loss today."

I still hadn't taken the ten. "Keep it," I say. "I just feel too lousy to care."

"No, you take it. Help pay for your newspaper ad with it, because that's a real good idea," and he puts the ten in my hand.

I go home. I phone the newspaper the next morning and put a notice in for the day after. Several people call about finding a pocketwatch, but none of them are mine. I put a second notice in the paper a few days later. This time nobody calls.

A week later Tom calls. He says "I saw your ad. You said you'd put one in, so I looked for it. Any luck?"

"No."

"That's too bad. You said in the ad you'd give a reasonable reward. Would you have considered three hundred reasonable?"

"That's twice as much as I wanted to give, but I probably would have."

"Would you still consider three hundred reasonable if you learned I'm the one who has your watch?"

"You were hiding it?"

"Whether it was hidden or I found it, what's the difference? You'll never believe me anyway. But three hundred. Say yes or no. If it's no, I won't bargain down and I'll also never bother you about it again."

"Yes. I'll get the money up some way. I'll borrow it from friends."

"Don't fool with me, Gene. I might not look it, but you got to believe that just staying alive the way I do I can handle myself okay. So don't bring cops when you come meet me. Do, and I'll either toss the watch across the street on the sly or say I found it after you stopped looking that night, and phoned you today for your newspaper reward. You can't deny I was still looking."

"I won't bring anyone."

He gives me the time, day and place. I tell him I can probably get the money by then. I borrow two hundred dollars from several friends and also take the last hundred out of my bank account.

I meet him on a busy street. He says "The money." I say "The watch." He says "Let's meet each other's hands halfway." I hold out the envelope of money. He says "Open it." I open it. He sees the money. He puts his hand in his pants pocket and feels around inside. "Oh my God," he says.

"Don't give me that."

"No, this time it's for real. It's gone."

"Come off it."

He smiles. "Of course it's not. You think for three hundred I wouldn't make sure the pocket's sewed?" He takes out the watch. It's mine. I give him the envelope same time he gives me the watch. He immediately turns around and walks away. "You bum," I yell after him. "You bum. You bum."

STOP

A car stopped. Man got out. "You there," he said. I dropped my package and started running. "Hey wait, where you running to?" He knew. He knew I knew. Car stopping, man getting out, motor still running, driver inside with his hands on the wheel, car door left open so the man outside could jump right back in. And the look. If I could see the driver's face, probably both their looks. But I didn't have the time to speculate on all this. Just keep running.

The car caught up with me a block later. They drove alongside for a few seconds, pointing and talking about how good a runner I was, seeming to enjoy a joke, for they both broke up. Then they parked about fifteen feet in front of me. I stopped. Both men got out. Motor still on, doors left open. "You there," same man from before said, approaching me, driver staying behind. "We only want to speak to you about something, so what's the rush?"

Standing in the middle of an intersection I had four ways to go. Back, to them, either sidestreet. Back they probably had another car coming by now. Left sidestreet ended in a school ballfield with a chain fence around it with the exits at the other side of it locked sometimes. Right sidestreet I'd never been on before and I ran down it. "Oh for godsakes," the driver said, "do you have to? We just ate." They got in the car. Drove slowly behind me. Then accelerated past and made a sharp turn onto the sidewalk in front of me right up to the building's steps, cutting me off. I couldn't stop in time and slammed into the car door, went down, got up, legs gave and I fell down again. The man in the right seat seemed shaken too.

"Did you have to turn so fast?" he said to the driver.

"I didn't want to be chasing him all day. Anyway, I immobilized him."

I jumped up. Both doors opened. I was stuck in a triangle made by the car door and front of the car and the steps. Two possible ways out were to climb over the hood—but the driver suddenly stood there with his arms out as if to catch me—or down the steps.

"Now please, just a minute of your precious time," the driver said, climbing over the hood. Other man shut his door and reached his hand out for me. I ran down the steps and pushed past the vestibule door. Door to the hallway inside was locked. "Hold up already," the driver said. "My stomach, my feet." I rang all the building's bells. The men started down the steps. I braced one hand against the hallway door and foot against the vestibule door so the men couldn't get in. A woman on the intercom said "Yes?"

"Let me in."

"Who is it?"

"Just let me in please. It's an emergency."

"Not until I know who it is."

"Police. There's a man we're after who just ran into your building and we want to get in without breaking down the door."

"That's still not saying who it is." The men were trying to push their way in. "I need proof. For this building, in this neighborhood, you have to."

"Look out your window. That's our double-parked car on your sidewalk. Now would we park like that if we weren't after somebody?"

"I have the back view."

I rang all the bells, keeping my hand and foot braced against the doors. The men were caving in my foot. I kept ringing the bells with my free hand. The woman kept saying who is it, she needs proof, will I please stop ringing if I can't give it as she's old, too lame to be walking back and forth like this, till she or someone else rang me in. The driver threw open the vestibule door and rushed to get to the hallway door with the man behind him practically falling on top of him, but I got it shut. The other man got up and rang the bells. I ran to the back of the first floor looking for a rear exit. There wasn't one. I ran upstairs. The men were in the vestibule. "Yes, police," the driver said into the intercom. "Precinct Seventeen, ma'am. Officer Aimily. Your local patrolman's Grenauer or Pace. Pace then. But we're after a man who just came in your building. That's our car outside." Someone rang them in.

"There's a back entrance?" he said to the other man.

"No, all the buildings on this side face the river."

"What do you mean—right on it? I thought we were a block away."

"Flush up against. From some of the back flats you think you're float-
ing in the ocean."

They started upstairs.

"The roof," the driver said.

"Oh damn, I forgot. They're connected."

"You stay on the street. I'll follow him."

"But your stomach. And you said your feet."

"I'll live. Call in for more. He comes out, grab him. Bat him to the
ground if he won't stop. I've had enough."

The driver continued upstairs. I knocked on the rear doors as I went
up. The roof was out of the question. Unless someone was working up
there on another roof or sunbathing in this cold. For all the roof doors
were locked from the inside. Once up there you had to keep the door
open with something to get back in. Way it was in my own building and
all the roofs I'd been on in this neighborhood and by fire law all the roofs
in the city. But if someone in one of the rear apartments opened up I
could run past him, throw open a back window and jump out and try to
swim away. I'd jump from two stories up at the most. That would be
about three to four stories up because there must be at least a floor or
two between the ground floor and water. The fourth floor was a little too
high to jump from though I might give it a try if I really felt lucky. But
from the fifth floor I didn't think I'd survive.

Nobody on the third floor rear opened. The driver was panting as he
climbed the stairs. I had youth on him, energy, not as much fat, no recent meal in me, not that any of that would help me much unless I
jumped and swam. Nobody on the fourth floor answered my door-
pounding either and I climbed the last two flights and unbolted the roof
door.

No stick or anything to wedge under the doorknob to keep the door
closed. Now the driver was climbing the last flight. "Boy," he said, resting halfway up and seeing me looking down at him, "you're the biggest
pain I've had all week. I could throw you off that roof—I'm not kidding.
Throw you off without thinking much about it for what you're putting
me through."

I looked around. "Anybody on one of the roofs here? Hey, do you
hear me, anybody around?" Nobody answered and I couldn't see any-

one. I ran to the next roof. They went on for a block. The last roof looked down on the street I'd just run on, the avenue where I'd first seen those men, and the river. The man stepped out onto the roof, put a brick he found inside between the door and jamb so the door wouldn't close all the way. I ran to the last building, hurdling the dozen or so two-foot-high parapets separating each roof.

He followed me, stepping over each parapet very carefully so he wouldn't dirty his pants. "Don't make it so tough for me anymore," he said from five roofs away. "Meet me at some halfway point. Or, if you want, I'll go back to the door we came out of and you can meet me there."

"I don't know what you want," I said, "so why do you keep coming after me?"

"You don't know, then why you so quick to run?" from three roofs away.

"I see two big men chasing me, I run, wouldn't you?"

"We didn't chase. We walked. We drove. We said where's the rush? We were very polite and showed no harm. You smacked into our car, we didn't smack into you. But let's talk about it downstairs. It's filthy up here and the air stinks from the incinerators and exhaust chutes."

He was on the last roof with me. I tried opening the door. Locked. What a fool I was not to have tried the doors on all the roofs I ran across. They were probably all locked but I shouldn't have been so sure. Though even if I got in one of them, probably nobody in the fourth or third floor rear apartments in that building would have opened up for me and there was still that other man on the street and by now probably a few more. I looked over the roof to the street.

"Don't jump. You say you don't know what we're after you for—well okay, maybe you're right and we're wrong."

"Who's jumping?" There were lots of men down there, most looking up, and double- and triple-parked cars. The street had been blocked off.

The man came up to within ten feet of me. "How about it now?"

He was getting his wind back but maybe I could run around him. Left or right—where did I have the most room to get by him?—when another man came out of the door held open by the brick and then other men came out of several doors. I ran to the side of the roof overlooking the river. A liner was out there. *Olympia* it said. Ocean liner. Going for a cruise. All white. People on the outside decks, probably with drinks in their hands and bundled up in warm coats and furs. It must have just sailed. Tugs at both ends of it pulling away from it now, so it was probably starting to get out of the harbor on its own. I waved to it. Took off my sweater and waved it. A yellow sweater. Probably easily seen. Someone waved back to me. Now several people were—more. I was sure it was me they were waving at, probably some with binoculars looking at me too. I waved harder at them and yelled "Hey, hey, have fun, a great journey," even if I knew they couldn't hear me from where I was. Then a whole long railing of them at the bow were waving and then another railingful at the back and it seemed people from the other side of the ship were coming to this side to wave too. They were happy to wave to someone at the start of their trip, even if it was maybe only for a week south to the isles. I know I'd be.

"You're not going to be rushing me and doing anything silly with that sweater now?" the man said. He stayed where he was but the closest of the other men was now only a roof away.

"I wouldn't," I said, still waving. "I don't want to hurt anyone and least of all myself when I know I didn't do anything wrong."

"Then let me put these on you and you'll come along. Because really, I'm getting more mad at you all the time."

"Granted." I put out my wrists. He handcuffed them. The closest man was almost right behind him now. I broke away and jumped over the roof on the river side, my hand holding the sweater which trailed above me. From the liner I heard this loud single human noise.

That should have done it but they had a couple of launches below in case I jumped. Biggest surprise was popping out of the water alive. All it took for them was a long pole with a hook at the end of it which they got around the chain of my cuffs. They dragged me to the launch, lifted me out of the water gently and rolled me over on my belly and two men sat on opposite ends of me as if I was a very dangerous but prize rare whale.

THE MOVIEMAKER

She calls and says "I hear you have a novel about us coming out in the next few months and I want to write a movie script from it."

"Fine by me. You have fifty thousand to spare?"

"I've nothing but enough to live poorly on for the next three months while I write the script, so I want you to sign over the movie rights to me for free."

"You joking? I worked two straight years on that book, doing nothing else. And my agent won't let me just give it away."

"Your agent will do what you say."

"Then I won't just give it away."

"Listen. I want the rights to my life, do you understand, or at least my life with you. It's a good story, our years together, with a wild beginning, lots of backs and forths and a slam-bang finish, and if the script of it sells I'll pay you a good sum for the rights to the book. Fifty thousand if that's the going rate for a novel. Sixty to seventy-five thousand if the script sells big, which I think it will. What's it called?"

"*You and Me.*"

"That's the title? I don't like it, for a movie or a book. For my script of it I'll have to come up with a much better title. Like *The Lovers.*"

"I think there was a title like that once for a movie."

"A French movie, years ago, two people making love in a bathtub if I remember the scene that almost cost it its license here. But my movie, which I'm also going to try to produce, will be definitely American. West Coast American with maybe a racy hot tub scene or just a quick almost subliminal shot of one if we want the rating to be PG."

"My novel takes place entirely in New York State and ends a little before the hot tub phenomenon caught on in the West. In fact the couple only leave Manhattan together twice. Once when she shows him her birthplace in the Bronx and the second time to the project her folks live in in Queens."

"Well, I've been thinking about it and her parents will live on a beautiful country or seaside estate in Baja or Southern California in my script. And if the main couple in the movie travel anywhere to see her birthplace, it'll be to some scenic city like Salt Lake or San Francisco, but one of those magnificently grandiose places like that out West."

"I don't see how they can leave this city's environs. It's a New York City book. One of the main points of it is that their lives are inextricably and to her, claustrophobically, bound by Manhattan, which is a recurrent argument between them. She wants to move to Westchester. He gets headaches and stomach cramps when he so much as thinks about going to one of the other boroughs for a few hours. He even remarks, two years into their affair, that he just realized they haven't been out of New York City since they met one another. At least he hasn't; she spends a few days in Dutchess County at a librarian's convention."

"That's what she does?"

"Why do you say that with such disgust? It's what you did before you took a couple of writing courses and quit the library system to write TV soap opera scripts. I thought of it as an unusual profession to make the principal female character. Also I learned so much about the technicalities of the work through living with you."

"I thought a book of fiction was supposed to be fictional or at least not that biographical that it reads like the writer's life as well as the lives and histories of his friends and family. Anyway, all that will have to be changed. I'm making her a newswoman for a local California television station and in my script the couple will think traveling and meeting different kinds of people is better than almost anything and so they'll be traveling a great deal. To Las Vegas. Lake Tahoe. Several High Sierra ghost and old gold towns and on to Mexico and bullfights and maybe even once to British Columbia and whatever's above that. Alaska. Why not? By propeller plane or helicopter or one of those tiny private jets. Over the highest peaks and low icy valleys and Eskimos on sleds and everything else you can see from the sky up there including the most gorgeous sunsets. Igloos if they still live in them. Polar bears and schools of seals. I want there to be plenty of traveling by car and plane and train, even, going on in my movie of your book. It's the cheapest type of film footage to shoot because you don't need sound or actors most times and the cameraman and director can go up in the plane alone to shoot the film or even buy some that's already been shot by a crew for an ad or documentary."

"I don't see how any of that's possible. Because in my novel John not only—"

"That's his name?"

"John and Dotty, yes."

"Dotty? Why not Dilly or Dopey? In my script they'll be called something a lot more exotic. Memorable names. Meaningful intelligent uncommon names. I don't know what. Lucinda I think I like best for the woman, though don't hold me to it, and for the man, perhaps Johann. And that's close to John."

"Why would he be called Johann? He's from New York City. Born, raised and public-schooled there and his parents and grandparents too."

"In the movie his folks will come from Switzerland or Scandinavia, and maybe Johann too, when he was three years old, which will explain why he has no accent. We can maybe even fly them to one of those countries for a brief visit to see his folks' graves. European camera crews and setups are much cheaper on a day-to-day basis than our own."

"His parents aren't dead."

"Listen, this is a movie. We only have an hour and a half, and with all that traveling in it, no time for elaborating every branch of the family tree. He gets a phone call. His parents are dead, the caller says. That takes five seconds. A quick flight to attend the funeral, courtesy of Swiss Air or Pan Am, whose insignia we'll show on the plane as it takes off and lands. At the gravesite he weeps, maybe Lucinda does too, and the phone caller, by their side now, whispers 'Car crash' or 'Double suicide,' with Johann nodding that he understands. One of his parents had terminal cancer and the other couldn't live without him or her. Or gambling debts or family disgrace. I'll work it out, and also how his folks got there: they moved back for their old age. Then dinner that night in an elegant restaurant in that country and a quick flight home. Denmark, we'll say. Dinner in Tivoli Gardens, which is such a pretty and cheerful place, so a startling visual and emotional contrast to his mournful face and sadness at the time. What's John in Danish?"

"Johann should be close enough. Look. Not to say I'm giving the novel to you, I still don't like the changes you're making. More you talk about it, more I think a novel should stay a book."

"What changes? Locations? Those have to be changed. It's cheaper making movies in California than New York. The unions and film processing charges and the rest are approximately the same. But more light. Less chance of rain or snow or whatever causing money-costing delays. And the names? Do yours have any special significance or symbolic intent?"

"No. John is simple and an everyman sort of name. What's more important is I thought they fit the characters."

"And their histories? Mine are fleeting, and more intriguing. People might want to read about poor and unsuccessful people, though I've my doubts there, but they certainly don't want to see them in the movies. And the title? Mine's better. *The Lovers* or *The Loved Ones*. We want to attract financial backers to the script, not drive them away. And lovers means lovers, period. Though for those who like probing for such things, my titles can be construed in various ways too, while yours can't. What's your book about other than us?"

"It's nearly three hundred pages and some very thickly written."

"To me, no matter how complex the work, if the creator can't summarize it in a single sentence, then I doubt he knows what he's creating."

"It's about language and love."

"What language? You mean all the arts and crafty tricks? Agglutination, polysyllabism, lyrical consonances and assonances and the like? That's what movies aren't about for sure."

"You're probably right and maybe that part of it can't be transferred to the screen. As for the story, very simply put it's about this couple, in their thirties, she's married, he's not, who fall in love, then she goes back to her husband—"

"You mean I go back to Ike."

"In the book he's named Bill."

"In the movie he'll be Raymondo or Raymond. That's what I always thought fit Ike best and wanted to call him. Do you include his almost inch-thick eyeglasses?"

"No. I thought he'd think I was poking fun at him."

"You should have used them. But maybe that affliction and our carrying on in the beginning when he's just about sitting on the same couch with us, can be put to better use in a movie than a book."

"Anyway, then you divorcing Ike or Bill and going back to John or me. Then you leaving me or John or Johann or even Johannes, which might be more Danish, for a much younger man who's a drummer in a jazz band. You still live with him?"

"No, I'm with someone else now, who's not as noisy—and you see? *The Lovers* is a perfect title. Or *The Loved Ones* or *Chain of Lovers*, meaning many lovers or loved ones and, if you want, the new kind of chains we put on ourselves by becoming so liberated and being so free with ourselves. And also the interminable chain of relationships and bedmates so many single and divorced people have today. What work does the man in your book do?"

"Writes novels."

"You can't make movies about fiction writers. To have him sit at a desk, alone, for hours, day after day smoking cigarettes and drinking coffee and every so often going tip-tap on his typewriter, or even worse, scritch-scratch with his pen when the mood strikes him, just isn't interesting to the moviegoer. And if he is a fiction writer and doesn't sit at his desk, the audience will ask itself when does he do his work? No, he'll be a television newswriter who talks about wanting to write a TV miniseries or sitcom show. That's where he meets her: at the station where she works, though her ultimate aim is to become the anchorperson of a network news show. In fact, while they're in Denmark for the funeral I'll have him sell the pilot for the TV series he's going to write. He can even get a phone call from Hollywood about it, again contrasting his depression over his parents' deaths with this unexpected professional success. Do I have children in the book?"

"I wish you wouldn't keep referring to her as—"

"Do I have children?"

"One, though I made him a girl. And as long as you insist my book is a facsimile of our lives: since John always wanted to be a father and husband, I gave myself two boys from a divorce several years before."

"I don't want either of them to be parents. Too many smart-mouth kids in the movies lately and I think the audience is tired of them or will be by the time this picture is released."

"Madelaine isn't smart-mouth in the book."

"That's the daughter's name? Might not be a bad one for the heroine of the movie. But definitely no children. For one thing, I don't write adolescent and teenage dialogue very well. For another, it's to be an adult movie only, so the children will have to be relegated to street shots and airport scenery."

"If it came to where no matter what I did to stop it you ended up with the rights to the novel, then use Madelaine's dialogue in it. I wrote it pretty well. Or have them hire me and I'll write new dialogue for it, but dialogue close to the characters in the novel. I might as well try to keep the movie as faithful to the original as I can, which includes its artistic intent, and I also wouldn't mind earning a big weekly salary for the first time in my life."

"You're to have nothing to do with the writing of it. It might even come to where not a word of your dialogue is used in the movie. At best, you'll eventually get a fat rights' check and one of those 'Based on the novel by' credits, which should help you get a paperback sale even if the hardcover and movie don't succeed financially or get decent reviews. One of the clauses of the contract I'm having drawn up for us is that the author of the novel has to stay completely away from the production and any decisions on the film."

"I'm not staying away from anything or agreeing to sign for any future fat fee if you're going to butcher my book."

"You don't understand yet. The book and the movie script of it are two distinct species. Some books, in fact, are bought solely for their titles or the publicity they got and the contents are discarded. But no matter whom the writer sells his book or title to for a movie, he never has anything to say about the changes made to his work. He takes the money and disappears, which is why the author—in your case this'll have to be a little delayed—gets paid so much for the rights to his book."

"Then I don't want to sell it to any movie company."

"You're not selling it to anyone but me, and only a two-year option at first and then for a much later fee."

"And if I don't?"

"Then I won't give you permission to publish the book."

"That's a bit late. Galleys have already been sent to the prepublication services, and the book's being printed and bound right now and should be out to the regular reviewers in a month."

"Then I won't let it be distributed. I'll have a restraining order imposed or something. I'll sue you and your publisher. I'll say you took our story and humiliated my child and me. You took Mallory and made him Madelaine. You took my name Doris and made me Dotty. You took my former profession and husband and made them hers. You even took my parents and probably their new apartment and my old one and probably my present street. Where does Dotty live?"

"Her last address is on West Twenty-fifth."

"Wonderful. I'm on Twenty-first. I won't even ask what avenues her building's between."

"They're different than yours, but not by much, and though she also lives in apartment 3F, her building's on the even side of the street."

"You're making my case. How old is Dotty and what years does the action take place?"

"She's thirty-five at the end of the book and it takes place between 1974 and 78."

"My exact age or thereabouts? And you don't think there were hot tubs in California then?"

"I never heard of them till a year ago. Not that if John had said in the novel what I just said to you, it wouldn't be plausible for the kind of person he is. Like me he rarely reads the papers, has no television set and doesn't keep up to date. Anyway, I'll have to speak to my agent about all this."

"Speak to her all you want. Have conferences. Speak to your editor and publisher and their legal people too. See if I can't cause a fuss. Also look at your book contract and see who has to pay the legal penalties and fees if they lose the suit. Not your publisher, I'll tell you."

"I'll look at it."

"Good. In the meantime I'll have my agent get the movie rights contract over to me by this weekend. Then I want you to sign it by the end of next week, as I don't want to give anyone else the chance to bid on your book. Because you know full well that just about everything in your novel isn't made up. It was taken from things we did. I've diaries from all those years, probably with many of the same things in them that are in your book. Did you get us making love in my school library the afternoon school closed for the summer and with the door, an anonymous note told us later, not locked enough to stop the custodian from walking in?"

"Yes I did. On the desk. Though instead of the start of the summer vacation I made it the Easter recess."

"It's in my diary too. Did you also put in the time when the city raised the subway fare overnight and we got so incensed at its sneakiness and double-dealingness that we leaped over the turnstiles into a policeman's arms?"

"Yes. Same station, maybe a different date. I made him a plainclothesman though, since I could never get it believable how we didn't see the policeman. But the incident's there. Couldn't pass it up. I won't deny it."

"You won't make a lot of legal trouble for yourself, will you?"

"I don't think so."

"You will give me, for a dollar, the movie option for the next two years, though with a more than fair property fee for you if I sell the film script?"

"I suppose I'll have to."

"You do believe, if you don't go along with me, that I'll contact your publisher and threaten to start a suit against you for violating my right of privacy and other things?"

"I believe you. No reason why I shouldn't."

"You know, when a friend said she saw the catalogue announcement and then the promotional description of your book and how much the synopsis of it seemed to parallel our lives, I went into an absolute depressive fit. Then I thought how much I could gain by the book being written and coming out. I've always wanted to write a film script about part of my life. I haven't had much luck with other scripts I've written or my soaps, though people in the business say I've a terrific talent for writing and all I need is the right story and a break. I thought about writing our story long before I knew you were publishing your book, but I just couldn't begin it, much as I tried. It was too personal a story. I was too close to it. People I love and loved could be hurt by it. All those reasons and more. But you wrote it. You're the professional writer, really.

You sort of did the beginning work for me. The rest should be reasonably easy. I'll change it where it suits me, sometimes when it's just too embarrassing to me and others to include, and also where the story needs a little more commercial input than I'm sure it has to sell as a movie. But you do write good dialogue. I didn't mean what I said about that before. And some of it—maybe lots—I'll probably keep in. You know, years ago when we first met I never thought our relationship would end, so much were we in love with each other, and when it started to, I never thought anything would come out of it to benefit me like this. But I'm sure, compulsive writer that you are, fervent to turn every living experience into a literary one if it happens to be convertible as such, you'll write a short story about this phone call, though also to recoup some of what you feel you lost by temporarily giving your novel to me for a dollar."

"I might. If I do and then send you a contract to waive all the movie rights to it, will you sign?"

"Only after you sign and return the contract for the movie rights to your book."

"Deal."

"What do you expect to do with the movie rights to a short story anyway? They usually can't be made into full-length films, and especially not one that's only about a long phone call."

"Who knows? Maybe I'll turn the story into a novel. All my novels started out as short stories and then just took off."

"If you do write a novel from the short story of this phone conversation, make sure it doesn't include anything you might have left out about us in the novel that's being published, or I might want the movie rights to that new book too."

"I'll remember."

"Then look for my contract in your mailbox next week," and she says good-bye and hangs up.

CY

One look at me, they turn away or run. All I have to do is step outside. Even leave my flat. Even begin to unlock my door and turn the doorknob: people in the hallway, they make tracks. Even the kids. Even the brave kids. The brave kids as fast as the most afraid though not as far. Once they've seen me. That's the ticket. The brave ones have to have seen me at least once. The bravest of the brave want to see me again and again. The most afraid take it from hearsay. Hearsay says: "Don't ever look at him. Face like a bogeyman, body even worse. Vampire, demon, hobgoblin, spook. The worst imaginations of hell." That's what I am to the most afraid. The bravest of the brave play a different game. They've got to get their jollies from being afraid. One flick of my lightswitch, and if they're waiting for me in the hallway as they like to do on rainy days: "Uh-oh, he's going out. Beat it, scram, scat, get. Doorknob's beginning to move. Here he comes. We'll watch out for you, we'll protect. There's his sleeve. There's his shoe and leg. Oh my God what a sight. Run. Run." Often I hear them around the corners of the staircase as I hobble down. Bad face, bad leg. For each of my steps down, they make one too. Though to some adults my face and posture might be interesting. Isn't that what they say? The uglier you are, the more interesting you become. Never met a person who felt that way about me yet. Nobody that courageous so far, maybe nobody that perverse. But I'm leaving the house. I don't really know what makes people tick. I'm more than taking a walk. I'm going to try to make today a very special day.

I lock my door. "Why lock it?" someone might say. If I'm as scary looking as I tell it, who'll want to go into my flat? Landlord, for one. With the super and a couple of drifters off the street hired as haulers for five dollars each. Maybe because it's my apartment: ten. Though each about to whiz in his pants, afraid I might suddenly return and catch them emptying out my apartment quick. Not that I don't pay the rent. I do. I've got a one hundred percent disability, which keeps me alive. Army wounds. That's where the initial disfigurement and the monthly money come from. Grenade went off near my face. Not an enemy grenade. Oh yes, the enemy, but not our country's. A soldier friend. Accused me of making it with his girl. Grenade practice. We were allowed ten duds, and then, when we had proved our aim and had been taught the safety musts of grenade tossing, one live one to heave at a target fifty feet away. He held it above his head. Said "Admit, admit," and I kind of jokingly said "I cannot tell a lie, Ed, I never so much as set a fingertip on your girl." I don't know why I didn't run or drop instead of standing there. Shock maybe. My best pal: a real grenade flying at my face? He timed it just right. Pulled out the pin, counted three seconds, tossed it at me and it exploded in midair. He was smart enough to throw himself to the ground and only got a few shrapnel bites in his ass. He learned his lessons well. But I just stood there: "I don't even know who your girl is," I think were my actual last words for several years. But the vocal cords were eventually patched up to a degree, and with a dozen plastic surgery operations, courtesy of the government, half my head and face, but there was too much to be replaced. But where was I? Can't say my mind wasn't also a little affected by the blast. Oh yes. Special day today. More than just taking a walk. Imaginary people invading my apartment to get rid of me if I don't triplelock the door. And the explosion, head and face injuries, and the body roughed up a bit though not as much as it was in my two other accidents.

Because being blind in one eye from the grenade explosion, I didn't see this bicyclist steaming down on me in the park one day. What he was doing on the pedestrian instead of the bike path is another story: one he always avoided telling. "I've been biking this park for years," he told the policeman while I was crying for mercy on the ground, "and never hit a soul or tree. I'm a champion cyclist, I've ridden in derbies and competed in the most grueling obstacle courses—fire, moats, nails—and never got a scratch, never damaged a bike, never came in less than second or third, so it had to be this nut who jumped in front of me."

Sure. I did that. Wanted to break a leg and hip in ten places and walk like this, with a hobble to the left and after each step the right foot's left in the air so long I sometimes stumble off-balance to the floor. Sure. Add to the weird gimp the face from the grenade, mix in the results of my third accident, and anyone can get a good picture of the fine figure of a man I am today. A car: two years ago: still blind in one eye, now slow of gait, hobbling across the street with the light turning from green to amber but not yet red—and even when it does there's still a few seconds' safety margin for the pedestrian—a car jumps the light and drags me one hundred feet on its fender with my face slapping and sliding on the pavement till it stops with its front wheel parked on my chest. But the driver in court: "I waited for the light to turn green, then seeing the coast was clear, shifted into first and slowly started to drive. Suddenly this man ducked under my wheels."

That's right. Every time I see a moving vehicle I go berserk. Kids zipping down the sidewalk on rollerskates I'm at my suicidal peak. Sure. But the judge said he could well understand it: "Man as deformed as that would certainly think of killing himself." And the witnesses: backed up whatever the driver said. Maybe I ruined the meals they just had or were about to have: mate or friend slaved all day at the stove: what a waste! Case closed. From the last accident I lost my other ear—whatever sound I get comes in through two eyesore slits—chest caved in, leaving me looking like a tilted question mark when I stand, and most of the good the plastic surgeons did to my face from the grenade accident got rubbed out or mashed in irremediably, they said, when I bounced and slid on the street, besides my losing all sensation for temperature changes and pain.

But why think about it? A mess. I see it now. People I pass on the street: one look's enough, yeck! Artificial limbs and transplanted kidneys we've plenty of, but heads? An ordinary face? Doctor's final opinion: "Wear one of those ski caps pulled down to your chin with two holes cut out for eyes"—why didn't he say "one"? The doctors can look at me though. Nurses wince a bit, but the doctors have seen it all and to them I'm a medical wonder, so they've got to take more than a peek. A textbook case they say: lucky to be alive. But the landlord still wants me out of the flat. What does he care about medical history: he gets a lawyer's letter made up and drops it in my box. "A welfare worker rented the apartment for you under false pretenses, since you know the landlord would never have rented it to you if you had asked for the place yourself. He also claims mothers in the building complain you're the cause of their children's nightmares, children complain you're the reason they can't study, train themselves or eat, fathers complain you frighten their wives and daughters and ruin business in their local stores and shops, so for the sake of the building, block and neighborhood we shall begin eviction proceedings against you, if you won't leave voluntarily, and if that doesn't work, you'll be thrown out on the street."

I believe it. I can understand it. I know I haven't much time left there, but where am I going to move? "Go to a nursing home," the super's yelled through my door. Why not an old age home: after all, I'm almost thirty-five. And I've applied. All the homes, but none will take me unless I consent to being locked in my room and never allowed out except when the rest of the patients are asleep, forfeit ninety percent of my disability check for the costs of being an outcast, and have my food shoved through a special chute built in my door. Thanks a lot. So I put up with the threats and gaff. I walk the streets. Today with a big purpose in mind. Today's the day I decided, yes sirree. My sole enjoyments up till now and for the past ten years: going to the park and watching the ducks quack and beg, the swans glide on the pond, the geese overhead. And the tots. They don't mind me. So freshly formed. They're not afraid of me at all. Their mothers are, though: snatching the kids away from me fast. And if they're pregnant again: afraid their unborn babies will look like me, so they summon the police: "That man," I've overheard. "That beast! That thing! That it!"

Who can go on like that? That's what I asked myself in bed today. Couldn't get up: thought I might just starve myself to death. But hope gave me courage to eat and leave the house. Hope's a doctor I insist exists somewhere on this globe who can do my face up a bit, improve my voice, which since the chest caved in has been hardly more than an intelligible rat's squeak, straighten the tilt a little as it'd be so nice to even walk just a trifle lopsided as I did after the grenade accident. Though some people: one never knows. Maybe for a day, a year, they'd like the power of a path opening for them as it so often does for me when I walk down a street. As is happening now. Like a path for a president, a czar, a great movie star, and maybe also someone with a year's run of unwashed body smells. I've seen it happen. Smelled is more accurate: my nose, though shaped like a corkscrew with a single nare, still functions okay. At a library: a lady like that. Suddenly the smell. I knew right off what it was: walking death. That's how we'll all probably reek one week in the grave.

But with her I think it was power. Really lapping it up it seemed. So blasé. Taking her time inspecting each shelf, but out of the corner of her eye watching the impression she made on the man who just passed, his fingers gripping his nose. Then she spotted me: another one who didn't wince. Buddies under the skin, I suppose she thought. Two power-houses meeting: dictators of our own domain: she of the odors; me, the looks. But I cleared out like the rest. Face: smell: no how-do-you-do's from me. And she's got a remedy I haven't got. Few successive scrub-bings and soakings and bury the clothes and she's as sweet as everybody else.

But here I am. I ring and walk in—just like the sign says—but the receptionist: one look and she gulps, gets up, turns around, pretends to file: "Sorry," she says, "doctor's not in. What I mean is . . ." still with her back: God, you'd think she'd have seen them all in a plastic sur-geon's office, "he's in, but busy. Appointment book's all filled up. Filled up for a month in fact. Then he's on vacation. If there's a cancellation before then. . . ." What's she talking about? Nobody's in the waiting room but me.

"It's urgent."

"With you it's always urgent. I know. I don't mean to be unsympa-thetic. It must be rough. But he's told me. Any new discoveries or de-velopments about your case, you'll be the first to know. He's promised. But there isn't another case like yours. You're unique."

I walk past her. With her back to me she won't even know till I've reached his office.

"Please, doctor. One minute's all I ask. I'm about to give up." He waves the receptionist away, points to a seat. "Surely something new must've been found in three months. Have you tried Russia, China, Af-rica, Japan? They're doing wonders with folk medicine now I've read. Acupuncture, then? Snake venom? Vitamin E?"

"We've tried," he says. "I've tried. There are no bones to break to correct your nose. Nothing to cover the ear apertures that wouldn't im-pair what hearing you have. Your missing eye socket's been leveled off. No supporting gums to sink a tooth or hold a plate." He goes on. My case history. "Half a skull . . . most of it reconstructed . . . by me . . .

a special cement . . . quarter of your brains gone also . . . yet here you are . . . reasonably alert . . . fairly good motor and muscular control . . . some vision . . . perceptible reflexes . . . all the hair and cilia out . . . that can never be explained . . . isn't important except cosmetically . . . but your gastrointestinal tract's fine . . . lungs and cardiovascular system couldn't be better . . . buck up . . . you'll live a normal lifespan . . . lots of people can't even say that . . . doctors don't know everything . . . maybe one day . . . fifty years from now the way science's been advancing . . . they'll know not only what kept you alive after your injuries but how to restore a patient like you to the original . . . but for now you're a medical phenomenon, a reconstructive impossibility."

"Vienna . . . Stockholm . . . Vietnam. Surely the doctors must have run across similar plastic surgery cases in Vietnam?"

"I've written, read all the journals, inquired at medical conventions. Nothing. Try wearing a much longer cap. Maybe I've suggested that. Or an eye patch. They can be quite chic, and I'm not saying that for a laugh. And move into a nursing home. I'll try to get you admitted to one. A life alone like yours can be unhealthy. But what else can I say? Get a dog."

I go home. My apartment's been broken into. All the doors are off. Furniture destroyed, mattress and linens soiled, clothes slashed. It had to happen one day. Landlord, tenants, neighbors: they can only take so much. Menace to the building, economic danger to the community: I understand. I'm sure the cop on the beat provided the know-how, the judge up the street the crowbar. What they don't realize is I can't leave. Find another place? Fat chance. Sleep on the sidewalk and get mauled by a do-gooding gang? Somehow I'll get a locksmith up here. Maybe that welfare worker can impersonate me again and let him in. For now, I'll curl up on the floor.

An ammonia bomb's thrown into the apartment. Then two more, till I get up, five o'clock I figure by the sky: evening graying into day, and yell out the window: "Okay. I know when I'm beat. Give me another hour's sleep and you've struck a bargain." Two more bombs are tossed in. I leave with only the clothes I've got on. And the savings book and cash I carry with me everywhere. And who's to complain to? Some federal agency about my civil rights? Sure thing. Mayor's office or Bureau of Consumer Affairs? You bet. And I know where to go now. Only one place left for me. The one I wanted to avoid most.

I knock on her door. "Yes?" she says.

"Mom, it's me. But before you open up—" Too late. "Son!" I hear. Then the door's being unlocked. I should've called first. Don't be surprised if I've changed a little, I would've said. The door's instantly slammed shut. "Imposter," she says. "Cyrus is dead."

"Not that easy, Ma. If you don't want to let me in that's another story, but remember the heirloom compote I broke when I was five? The dog called Bo I loved so much and buried in the backyard? The time Dad took us to the aerodrome show and three planes collided above our heads? Do you still have the souvenir that floated down from the sky into your lap? And the old jalopy we had painted black from blue? Remember its rumble seat you wouldn't let me ride in till I was six? 'On your sixth birthday,' you always said. 'Not till Cyrus's six.' "

"Not true. We could never afford a car."

"And here's one you couldn't've forgot. Who taught me how to walk?"

"I did. I mean, I taught my son how to walk. A mother usually does."

"It was cousin Ferdie. Ferdie who was studying to be a physical therapist and got killed in the last great war. Everybody thought something was wrong with my legs. I was already three and a half and still crawling. Maybe it's his head, people said. A retard . . . a basket case. But Ferdie said 'There's nothing wrong with him. Watch,' and he said 'Cyrus want candy?' I shook my head. Nodded, rather. That's another thing. A selected short subject. You were always teaching me the difference between nod and shake. 'Shake is to no,' were your words, 'nod is to yes.' But the main feature's my first steps. Ferdie went across the room and said 'Here, Cyrus, you want to have candy, you walk across the room. One step you get one piece. Two steps, two. Walk all the way to me and you get the whole jar. All yours to eat when you want to and as much as you like.' You protested. Said I could get cramps eating a whole jar of sourballs at one time. But Ferdie said 'You want him to walk, he'll walk. But Cy's got to have your approval about the candy first.' Dad said 'If it's jake with Cyrus, it's jake with us.' I walked straight across the room to pick up my prize. Didn't falter once. That's what you said later. 'You never faltered a second, as if you were born not only to walk but to run. To skip and be a champion racer and soccer player and do anything with your feet. Even dance. You'll be a great stage dancer one day,' you said. And remember how sick I got that night with all the candy I ate and you—"

"Cyrus," she says. "I thought you were dead." She opens the door. Her eyes are shut. And lets me hug her. My first hug in how many years? Her arms stay held out behind me, as if she's still waiting for someone to come into them. But I'm there. "Oh, Ma, can you ever know what this moment means to me?" Her eyes stay closed. Her nose is pinched. Maybe she thinks everything inside me also went haywire. But it is a hug. I don't dare kiss her cheek yet. I kiss the air instead. I've forgotten what it's like to hold another human being. The feeling can't be physically or mentally reproduced. How often I've hugged my pillow. Myself, if only to embrace some person's flesh. And even though she doesn't hug back, the feeling can be the living end. Not even a dog have I kissed the nose of or hugged in ten years. Before today I would've given half my savings to hold or nuzzle a child for a minute or less. Not just to touch someone. I've bumped into plenty on sidewalks and in the subway and department stores. Sometimes on purpose to feel what they still feel like after a very long while. Most times accidentally: in their frenzy to get around me we'd clunk shoulders or nick hands. But an honest-to-god hug? It all comes back. When I used to freely hold and hug people: women, girls, boys. In kindergarten. In grammar school. Teammates hugging the daylights out of me after we won the state championship. When I was in the army. Not my friend's girl. I didn't touch her. Why couldn't he take my word? I did know her, but only to talk to as a close friend. I thought he'd get mad if I told the truth. Ed had a reputation on the base as an excitable jealous man. And what's happened to him? Married her of course. They had children, he became a famous outfielder: peg to home like a rifle shot from three hundred fifty feet away. Then divorced and remarried to a showgirl and more children: I read about him in the newspapers and magazines. A sock on the jaw was all I deserved. That should've been the extent of his rage unless I'd raped her.

The hug's over. She turns her back, says "Come in, but quickly." Already the change in attitude, the urgency in her voice: people across the street will think she's cohabiting with the devil. "Sit here. You hungry?" She gives me a sandwich and milk. Her eyes always away or closed. Food on a paper plate, milk in a disposable glass. Will she burn the napkins I use, scour the garbage pail daily? Maybe she thinks what I've got is contagious and because we're blood her chances of getting it are twice as great. She does say, which nobody's said: "It'll take time. You have to excuse my behavior, but I'll adjust to you yet. We'll do something to change your condition. A mother can work miracles for her child. I'll see doctors."

"I've seen them all. Zero can be done. And I don't want to hurt you, ruin your life in this town. But not even a fleabag hotel would take me in. 'Sorry: all booked,' though they were starving for guests. I did have the train car to myself all night. And could've ridden free: the conductor never came in to punch my ticket. So there are advantages being like this. But I'll only stay the night. If you still don't mind me in the morning, then two nights. Always from day to day though, and whenever you say go, I'll go."

"Never. You're my flesh and blood. My only child. Your poor father. Good thing he's dead. I'm sorry, but good thing for you too, as he never would have tolerated your being here. Bad for business he would have said. For his heart, our community standing, the family name. But I'm glad you saw to coming home. You knew there was always your mother. Silly as this might sound to you: a mother never stops loving her child and is the only one who'll welcome him back into her house no matter what's happened to him or what he's done outside."

That's true. I say good night. No more hugs. I could've used one more. But my old room. Mom's kept it up. Pennants of my old schools. The trophies and awards I won. My legs were as good as she'd predicted. I excelled in all sorts of sports with my quick movements, long strides, record-breaking speed. High hurdles. Sixty and one-hundred-yard dash. A halfback. Shortstop. Crack of the bat, my bat, and zzzing the ball went, I went, whipping around the bases, stretching doubles into inside-the-park home runs. And the pictures: me with my best girl, my graduating class, Simonizing my first car, and about to enter college, when the army stepped in. Well: who didn't it affect? And even my medical discharge framed. Army must've sent it to her at her request. So she knew something was wrong. She probably even asked after my injuries, but what could they say? Cranial disjunction? Ophthalmic dysfunction? Rhinoplasty: surgeons did their best. And the one hundred percent disability, since they knew I'd never find work. I tried. After a few hundred turndowns, I even applied to circuses and traveling sideshows. Send us photos they said: "Grotesqueness is our butter and bread." So I got some photos in a four-for-a-quarter machine. Once stripped down in a half-dollar booth to really give them a look. Curtain drawn: nobody saw. Not that a big courtroom to-do with judge and jury and then imprisonment would have bothered me that much: but I'm sure I would've wound up in a solitary cell as in a nursing home. The few freak shows that answered my applications were very honest: "Too grotesque. There's got to be a middle ground in every profession. If you've no limbs then you've got to have a pleasant face and do a trick with the stumps like type or play the harmonica, though we don't ask for concert hall expertise. We're here to startle and thrill the audience, not infuriate and disgust them where they want to tear down the tent. Thanks for trying us though, and good luck." The ones who wrote back did so with more respect and consideration to me than anyone since the army. They know how tough it is getting jobs in their line of work and the lonely outcome and near-poverty circumstances for the applicants who are too extreme for the norm. And it wasn't just to make money and be with some understanding people and feel like I was chipping in with society as a whole by serving myself up as entertainment that I wanted the job. But also to try and have a close relationship with a woman who'd be physically equal to me, and I thought the sideshow would be the best place to meet someone like that. For there's nothing I or the doctors know of that's diminished in my erotic and emotional parts. But enough of that. Instead I make love and declare my positive intentions to the women who fill up my dreams. One can almost say I live to sleep—and for the faint hope that in the near future my physical condition can be changed. In my dreams I am always the man I was before the grenade.

My bed's nicely made. Sheets clean and smooth, pillows aired and plump: it'll be my most restful night's sleep in years. But a few hours into it something wakes me up. A movement in the room like little cautious feet. There can't be any rodents in my mother's house. Maybe a pet she didn't speak of has come to lick my face or nap in its traditional place under the bed. I turn on the light. It's my mother with an axe that's swishing down at my head. I move: it cuts into my neck. There goes another piece: thank God from the waist up I'm mostly paralyzed. I roll to the floor: her second chop slips into the sheets. I grab the axe from her and drop it out the window. Now to see how bad's the cut.

I wrap my neck with a towel. "Knot this for me please," I want to say, but something to do with my vocal cords must've got stuck. *Tie this*, I write on paper, *before I bleed to death*.

"I can't, son, don't you see? There's no place in the world for a boy like you."

Call the hospital, goddammit!

She leaves the house. Could be to get the axe. I dial Emergency. When he says "Officer Peters: what is it?" I tap an SOS on the receiver with the pen. "Is there something wrong? Will you stop making noise and speak? If there is something the matter, how will I know where to reach you if you can't say what's the address?"

Maybe if I keep tapping SOS someone else will get on the phone and understand and start tracing the call. But here's Mom again and as I figured: going to finish the job. I cup my hands in prayer, wave for her to stop, write *Listen, let me be the one to decide when to put an end to it*, but the axe is swung at my face.

I push her up against the wall with a table and head for the door. Behind me she says "Spare him. Help him. Make him to understand the depth of a mother's anguish."

I pound on her neighbor's door. I can predict their reaction, but I've got to take the chance. On a paper I've written *Call for an ambulance: there's been a serious accident*. The door opens. From her front yard my mother yells "Watch out: that animal tried to brutalize me." The man shouts for his gun. A woman comes running downstairs. He shoots one over my head. "Out out out," he says. All the lights in the neighborhood are now on. Anyway: someone's bound to call the police. I go into the woods that face these homes to wait for them. They'll take care of my wound: policemen have strong stomachs. Then the ambulance, hospital, an investigation: somehow I'll prove I'm my mother's son and who tried to brutalize whom.

I hear sirens. A policeman: "How long you say he's been in there?" Time to come out. But my mother: "I never saw him before he attacked me with an axe. This axe. I wrenched it from his hands. He's heavily armed. Guns, knives, he talked of explosives around his waist." What to do? Further into the woods for a mile till I reach another development with more men with guns in their homes and calls to the police? I couldn't even hobble a half block with this gash. And start for the police and they might shoot me before I could explain. Well, I should at least try. Don't want to stay here and just die. There's always the future if they don't kill me straight off. The possibility of new discoveries: I still insist. Why not plastic ears, eyes and noses in twenty years and simple injections that clear up all blemishes and illnesses inside and out? Or a sideshow that'll finally have to hire me because of a lagging, jaded audience and want of anything more grotesque. The middle ground can also change. Maybe this last blow did the trick. And there are always the tots to watch. The ducks, swans and geese overhead. I've got no pain. I don't ask for much. My mother, after ten more years of my scrounging, might even mellow toward me and take me back. I crawl to the lights I vaguely see.

"I think he's coming," a policeman says. "Throw out your weapons and leave your explosives behind."

If I could speak I'd say "Help, I surrender, dear." Something like that. But instead I stand and put up my arms and wave my pajama top.

"It's him, it's him, all right," my mother says. "And he said he especially hates policemen and will shoot them on sight."

THE SHIRT

For a few months I've been helping the man who lives in the apartment right below mine. I didn't have to help him before, except for maybe carrying up heavy packages for him, but then he had a stroke that left him slightly paralyzed on one side and blind in his right eye. So when I see him on one of the landings I always assist him up or down the stairs. Or when he hears me going downstairs, no matter how lightly I might sometimes try to walk, he'll say from behind his door "Michael?" and I'll say "Yes, Mr. Bricker" and he'll say "Could you hold up for a moment, I'm afraid I've another favor to ask of you." He usually wants me to get his mail or a newspaper or a few emergency groceries. If I'm going out and won't be back for a few hours, he'll still give me change or his mailbox key and say to leave the newspaper by the door or slip the mail and key under the door when I return. He occasionally says after I've done him a favor "I'll catch up with you later," but he never has. Not that I want anything from him. He's retired and ill, seems to just get by on his social security and a pension, and none of the things he asks of me take that much time or are that hard or complicated to do.

Today when I'm passing his door he says "That you, Michael?"

"Yes, Mr. Bricker."

"Hold up for a moment, and it's not a favor I want this time."

I wait. Though he sits near the door reading or watching TV most of the day, it still always takes him a minute or so to open it.

He opens the door and says "I said it wasn't a favor I wanted and I meant it. I have something for you for being so kind to me these past months."

"There's no need, really. I'm more than happy to do what I can for you."

"I know that but please don't deny me this little opportunity to repay you. Whatever it is I got here, it's small in comparison to what I'd like to give you if I had the means." He's been keeping something behind his back and now produces it. A shirt in a transparent plastic case.

100

"I'm sure it's your size and I think you'll like the style. It's from Formosa and takes nothing to wash."

"Polyester?"

"A hundred percent. Wash it when it gets filthy and hang it up and I
guarantee it'll be dry in an hour and look like it came from the French
cleaner's. I have several myself. That's why I never asked you to take a
shirt to the laundry for me, not that I've anywhere to go."

"Honestly, I've more shirts than I need, though thank you," and I
hold it out to him.

"Now you listen to me, mister. Big as you are and weak as I've become, I'm still strong enough to knock you off your feet with one fist, so
you're to accept this gift whether you like it or not and wear it, you understand?"

"It's really a very nice shirt and I thank you."

"Believe me, I'm the one who has to thank you a hundredfold. Because you won't know till it happens to you, God forbid, how terrible
it is to be afflicted and made so helpless like this. So when you give me
your help from time to time, I appreciate it more than you could ever
know."

I was on my way to my mother's for dinner, but I'll have to leave the
shirt in my apartment first. Though maybe she knows someone to give
it to—her super or the husband of one of her friends. But just so nobody
on the subway will think I stole the shirt, I fold it in half and carry it under the book I've with me.

It's an hour's ride and a ten-minute walk to her apartment building.
We kiss at the door and then she pushes me back into the hallway and
says "Guess who dropped in for the year uninvited and without a single
phone call?"

"Uncle Rolph?"

"Straight from Florida in his behemoth car which there's no space
around large enough to park in, to do business here he says, though if
he leaves my dinner table once in the next two weeks it'll be a miracle.
He doesn't look good, though, so pretend he looks better."

Rolph comes out from the living room in bright green pants, yellow
golf shirt, white belt, alligator shoes and a big cigar he puffs on and

clouds up his part of the hall just before we shake hands. "How you doing, sonny?"

"Fine thanks." We go inside. "I don't know how you feel, but you certainly look good."

"Think so? The pipe here," and he raps his chest, "killed me the entire drive up. Probably indigestion. That highway food in the South's too greasy and spicy. What've you got there, another book?"

"Sure, still reading, but also a shirt." I bring it out. "Too large for me but it might fit you. Made in Formosa."

"Since when they make good shirts there?"

"I don't know. The neighbor who gave it to me for doing him some favors seems to know something about shirts and he was impressed when he said it was from Formosa. You're a big guy in the shoulders. Could you get into an extra large?"

"That's my size. It's for sure not yours. Some gift this guy gave you."

"You mind polyester?"

"If I do then I got to be crazy. Because if you go in my bathroom in Florida that's all you'll find is polyester shirts drip-drying over the tub. Think I'd wear one of those cottons or even a cotton blend and walk around in wrinkles?"

"You could take them to a hand laundry," my mother says.

"What, at almost a dollar a shot to be shrunken and discolored and the buttons knocked off? No thank you." He takes the shirt out of the case. "Nice bag it comes in too. Strong plastic. Not like ours. You could use it to store the shirt later on." He holds up the shirt. "I like it. Just my kind of style. Not jazzy or button-down collar but nice. Offer still on?"

"You sure you want to give it away so soon after you got it?" my mother says.

"Mom, I want to give a shirt, let me give a shirt. I know what I'm doing."

"But you haven't even tried it on yet. It might say extra large but be a large. And it's a present and brand-new and you need shirts. Look at the one you have on. It's clean but I see you in it almost every time you come here."

"In the summer you do. Winter and fall you see me in two other shirts and spring maybe one or two more. I have five shirts and that's enough."

"Five for every occasion?" Rolph says. "Should I tell you how many I have?"

"Probably a lot more."

"Maybe two hundred."

"Stop," my mother says.

"Stop what? I'm not saying *exactly*, but two hundred shirts and two hundred suits and fifty sport jackets and maybe sixty pairs of shoes and plenty of ties, watchbands and belts and the like and I don't know how many pairs of slacks. Maybe fifty too. Maybe seventy."

"Where do you keep them all?"

"He needs two apartments," my mother says, "but only has one. I remember what his place looked like that one time I was there, so I don't see why I acted so surprised. He wanted me to take his bedroom and he'd sleep on the living room couch. I ended up in a hotel that night. Because not only were shirts hanging over the tub and sink but he had a coatrack in the bathroom with suits and things on it in zippered bags. And because all his closets were filled tight, these same kind of racks in every room. And under the bed which was too uncomfortable to sleep on because of this, suitcases packed with clothes. And piled on top of the bed and dressers and couch and desk, maybe fifty to sixty more jackets and spring coats and suits. You must sleep out with women every night, Rolph, because I don't see where there's any room to sleep home."

"I won't say I'm too old to still be with a woman."

"You won't say. I'll remind you what mother used to say. 'There's no fool like an old fool,' but not to get away from my main point, you're a clotheshorse, Rolph."

"And proud of it. Look, some people have a drinking sickness, right? Cognac. Wine. Everything. They die from drink. And some people eat all the time and die of heart diseases or if they make two quick steps, the heat. Me, it's clothes. Do I suffer? Does my body suffer? Does anybody suffer? Absolutely not."

"Your wife left you because you spent too much on clothes," she says.

"Not because of that. Because of other things."

"It contributed, or had to."

"So a little. So big deal. So who cares. The hell with her."

"What a way to talk."

"But she walked around in nothing. I was ashamed to be with her."

"Not nothing," she says.

"Mike, teach your mother something. No," he says to her, "not naked, but in rags. She dressed awful. She looked like a ragpicker. Worse. Ragpickers at least wear some of the clothes they pick out of trash cans and don't sell. She wore clothes that were worn, wrinkled, mended and old."

"I never knew," she says.

"You never knew like you never knew I had two hundred suits. You knew."

"I didn't. As for your clothes, I knew you had lots of them, but not that many. Who does?"

"Maybe two hundred and twenty-five suits. When I go into a store and see a suit I like and it comes in three different shades I like and I can't make up my mind—"

"Don't tell me."

"Right. But I wear all three. It's good for me and looks good for my business."

"What business? You haven't been in business for years. You do just about nothing, so why do you need so many clothes? You drive up, drive back, drive round and around and maybe think about business during all those drives and trips, but what business do you do?"

"Don't say that, because it's not true. I still import and design and sell shoes."

"Where?"

"From my apartment."

"You store five million articles of clothing and accessories there and still have room to conduct a business? I know where one desk is—under a ton of clothing—but where's the other? On the terrace?"

"If you want to know, the shoes *are* mostly on the terrace. In specially designed airtight and waterproof boxes and crates."

"I give up. You say you do what you do, then you do, not that I fully believe you yet. What do you say we all have a drink."

"I'm going to change first. That's another reason I like plenty of clothes. So I can have them fresh on me a few times a day." He goes into the guest room.

"I'll say this much for him," she says. "He did come here with four enormous valises. One week he says he's staying here, but—"

"Maybe one week, maybe longer," he says from the guest room.

"Maybe," she says lower to me. "He drives me crazy. Only here one day and talk and more talk and most of it lies. All my brothers are such sad fools. My father did it to them. He was too strong—no feelings. Acted like an archduke. But how are you? I'm glad you could come."

"By the way," Rolph says from his room.

"Yes?"

"Not you—Michael. Thanks for the shirt."

"My pleasure," I say.

My mother's shaking her head. "He needed an extra shirt as much as you didn't. I'm sure there's still time to change your mind if he doesn't already have it on."

"Really, the shirt's not for me."

Rolph comes out in a white shirt and a tie and different pants and shoes. We have drinks, dinner, sit around and chat a while and I go home.

A few days later when I'm walking downstairs Mr. Bricker says "Hello, Michael. Did the shirt fit?" His door's wide open and he's sitting at the kitchen table next to it.

"Perfectly. It's a little too warm to wear now, but I will in the fall."

"What are you talking about? It's a summer shirt."

"Is it? I thought it was long sleeve."

"Short sleeve. You didn't open it?"

"I did quickly, but didn't unpin it."

"Would you prefer a long sleeve? You do, I'll take it back when I go to the store again and exchange it."

"Maybe I can exchange it."

"No, I get out, I can do it. And it's not really a store but a jobber I know who sells me the shirts at almost cost. But is extra large really your size? Now that I get a good look at your torso, you hardly seem big enough for a large."

"I'm actually pretty stocky in the chest. And my arms are long—a thirty-four or -five."

"By the way, Michael, you know anything about fuses?"

"Why, you need one changed?"

"You don't see me sitting in the dark?"

"With all the daylight in your place, I assumed you were just sitting with the lights off and door open because it's much cooler that way."

"It'd be a lot cooler if my fan worked. That's what blew the fuse. I'd get the super, but knew you were here and maybe coming down any minute and that you'd do it in a much nicer mood than he."

"What is it, the wires? Let me see."

I look at the fan. It needs a new plug. The fuse in his apartment's good, so I change the one in the basement, buy a plug at the store and replace the old one. The lights are on and now the fan.

"Boy, that feels good," he says. "I should have got you two shirts when I had the chance."

"One's more than enough. And because it's drip-dry, I can wear it almost every day if I want."

"Now you got the idea. But I still should have got you two. I still might."

"Please don't. I'm more than happy with what I got," and I go downstairs.

My mother phones that night. "You won't believe this," she says. "I saw Rolph leaving the apartment this afternoon with about fifty cartons of cigarettes for his ex-wife's sister and brother-in-law. He bought them in North Carolina on his drive up. Cheaper taxes, though they reimburse him for the cartons and I think a little something for his time. Anyway, in one of these four giant shopping bags is, what do you think? Your shirt. So I asked him 'What's that in there?' and he said 'Cigarettes. I would have picked some up for you but didn't know your brand.' 'You didn't know I smoke Mores?' I said. 'Mores?' he said. And did I know they're only made of vegetable matter and no tobacco, not one shred? That's why they're so low in nicotine and tars. I told him that's ridiculous and what I mean about what's in that bag is that shirt. 'What's it doing there?' I said."

"The shirt I gave him?" I say.

"The shirt I told you not to give and then to get back. You were so quick to get rid of it I could have killed you. Because when did he ever give you anything?"

"How do I know?"

"Never."

"Not even when I was a kid?"

"Never. Even your bar mitzvah he didn't give you anything, and he came with his wife, daughter and mother-in-law. I remember. You had a gift list."

"Please, let me try to forget that list."

"Why? You were more sensible then than you are now. And his name was the only one you didn't check off against the names of the guests for a cash or non-cash gift. Anyway, he said to me that the shirt didn't fit him, so he was bringing it to his ex-brother-in-law."

"I thought he said he was an extra large."

"He is or he isn't or he never was, which is my point. He only took it from you to give to his brother-in-law so they'd think he was a terrific sport. I told you he was a chiseler. By now you ought to know that all my brothers are."

"No they're not. And Rolph's all right. Did he at least try the shirt on?"

"I asked him that and he said he didn't have to. That some shirt manufacturer friend told him the other day that all Formosan shirts run much larger than their size. So you know what I did?"

"What?"

"I took the shirt out of the shopping bag. He said what am I doing? I said 'Rolph, if you can't use it, don't give it to someone who means nothing to us. Because maybe Michael knows someone to give it to.' "

"I don't. So let him do what he wants with it. It's a cheap ugly shirt, not my style or size or anything else, and I don't want to hear any more about it."

"No. He fooled you and he fooled me and besides, I don't want him getting away with everything. He comes here, eats and sleeps and gets entertained with my food and liquor for several days to maybe seven weeks and never takes me out or buys a pint of milk for my place which he does almost every night for his ex-in-laws and some woman friend he knows from years back, and you say I should also let him have the shirt? No. That's my way of getting back at him."

"Why not just tell him how you feel?"

"He's my brother. I don't want to hurt him."

"You don't think you did by taking back the shirt?"

"That he understood. He's smart enough to know that everyone draws the line somewhere, and that was mine. But telling him to take me out for dinner or buy a bottle of scotch or just leave here for good, which is what I really want, no. In some ways he's very artistic and too sensitive, and it'll end up hurting me. Anyway, whenever you come here next, I'm giving you back the shirt."

"What about Uncle Leon? They visit you every other Tuesday, right? He's even bigger around the chest than Rolph, so give the shirt to him. He's who I should have given it to in the first place."

"That's what I'll do, but after Rolph leaves."

"Actually, it's not a good idea. If Rolph sees it on him next time he's here, he might really take it bad."

"He has no memory, my brother. And if he does question Leon on it, I'll tell them the first shirt you gave to a good friend. And the second one you bought because you liked the first so much, but for some reason that one also didn't fit, so you gave it to Leon for doing me so many favors over the years."

"I already told Rolph I didn't like the style."

"Then you didn't buy it for yourself the second time but for other people. For them you thought it was nice—bright and summery. Just let me do what I want about this, all right?"

"If you want."

"And you'll also come next Tuesday when Sissie and Leon are here, okay? I'm expecting you."

I go to her apartment that Tuesday night. She greets me at the door and says "Rolph left for Florida early today. He wouldn't even stick around to see his own sister and brother-in-law after a year. How are you?"

"Just fine. Did Leon like the shirt?"

"The shirt? Don't mention it to them. You know what they did today?

Sissie and I went to the bakery and I bought a dozen and a half onion and plain rolls—"

"What do you need so many for?"

"For today and tomorrow and to freeze and you'll see. I bought a dozen and a half and she bought a half dozen for them. We come home and she immediately puts her rolls in her shopping bag and they both eat my rolls with their lunch. Then around three Leon says he's hungry again and so does she, so I say 'What would you like?' and they both say 'How about one of those delicious rolls?' Mind you. Not one of their delicious rolls, which are the same as mine and by this time probably even fresher, being in both a bakery bag and a plastic shopping bag, but one of mine. So I set out more rolls and they have one each and another between them and that leaves me with four left, because six are already in the freezer. Well, we're waiting for you, as usual you're late, so Leon has a drink and has to have another of my rolls to stave off his hunger, as he puts it, and also so the liquor won't rush to his head. Now, is that nice?"

"It doesn't sound it."

"Be honest. It sounds selfish and cheap. Not only are my brothers all chiselers but I'm beginning to think also my sisters and brothers-in-law. The hell with all of them."

"You're sounding just a little like Rolph now, and you're also speaking too loud."

"Don't worry, they're way in back. And if I sound like Rolph it's because in some ways he's right. He has no use for those two also, that's why he drove off before they came."

"Maybe you shouldn't entertain so much."

"What choice do I have? They come every other Tuesday."

"Tell them to come every third Tuesday if it's too much for you."

"It would sound too odd, every third Tuesday, and we'd get so mixed up with that schedule that they'd never come here at all. Besides, it wouldn't be polite. They'd take it badly. But whatever you say tonight, nothing about the shirt. Then, when you leave, take it with you and try and fit into it. Maybe it's a small extra large. Who knows how they tailor things in Formosa? Not Rolph, and he's full of it with his manufacturer friend. Maybe it's even a medium. If it's not, give it as a present to someone, but not to any of my brothers or brothers-in-law."

"I wish you hadn't taken it out of Rolph's bag. I wish you hadn't gotten me involved in it like this. Why do you make such little things into big ones? I wish you'd have just stayed out of it, Mom. Really, you shouldn't have intervened at all."

"All I've just told you and you still don't think I was right?"

"Let's forget it."

"No. You still don't think I was right?"

"If you talk much louder they'll hear you no matter how far back they are."

"Let them. I want them to. Maybe from now on they'll eat some of their own rolls here and not save them all for home while they deplete mine."

"Mom, you're too worked up, there's no talking to you now. Excuse me," and I go past her, through the living room into the kitchen, kiss Sissie's cheek, shake Leon's hand, and make us each a drink.

"You're gaining weight," Leon says after we toast.

"I've actually lost five pounds this summer," I say.

"Could be the clothes you wear," Sissie says. "They droop so."

"I don't like tight pants or shirts."

"I wish he would," my mother says, coming into the room. "Or any kind of shirts but the ones he wears. They're all old and worn."

"Shirt he has on looks okay," Leon says.

"In fact it looks like a very nice one," Sissie says. "All cotton?"

"Yes," I say.

"You always liked them. I can see why. They're nice to touch. I can't wear anything but synthetics during the summer. They're light."

"They itch on me."

"Michael has a very nice light synthetic shirt he left the last time he was here," my mother says. "Someone gave it to him. An elderly neighbor for all the helpful things Michael's done for him. Why don't you put it on, Michael?"

"I'm not fifteen again, Mom."

"Just to see how good it might look on you."

"It won't look good. Certainly not on me. Nor will it feel good either. In fact—"

"If you say anything, Michael. . . ."

"Say what?" Sissie says.

"She thinks I'm going to try to leave it here again," I say.

"That's what your mother meant?" Leon says.

"I think so. I'll take it home, Mom, so don't get excited."

"Rip it up for all I care," she says. "But you should take it home. You need shirts."

We have dinner, sit and talk, and when we're ready to leave my mother sticks what's left of the dinner into containers for me and puts the containers and the shirt into a shopping bag. We kiss her good-bye and walk to the subway.

"I saw the shirt your neighbor gave you," Leon says. "It's a beauty. Why would you want to forget it every time you go to your mom's?"

"I just don't like it, though I'll probably get used to it."

Sissie says "Used to polyester to someone who hates polyester and is so pure with his all-cotton clothes? I don't think so."

"What size is it?" Leon says. "I only got a quick glimpse, but it looked plenty wide."

"Extra large."

"You? An extra large?" Sissie says. "Leon's an extra large and look how much bigger around the belly and chest he is than you."

"My mom wants me to keep it, so for her sake I will."

"That's the best way," Leon says.

"I'm not sure. Maybe you should have it. Yeah, I want you to, Leon."

"No no, really, I couldn't."

"Take it," Sissie says. "He wants you to have it and it's obviously no good to him."

"No, it's too nice and new. It's not even that. Mike doesn't have enough shirts, and Paula wants him to keep it, so he'll get used to it like he says."

We enter the subway station and I take the train back to Manhattan.

Mr. Bricker's door is open when I walk upstairs. "Michael, I know it's a little late, but can I ask you to do something for me again?"

"If you do something for me first."

"Anything, so long as it's nothing physical."

"I'd like you to take back your shirt." I take it out of the shopping bag and give it to him. "No hard feelings. It's a very nice-looking shirt. But strange as this must sound, I wore it for just a minute and it itched like crazy. It turns out I'm allergic to synthetic textiles to the point where I sometimes get a rash. I appreciate your giving it, but the shirt really doesn't work for me."

"No problem. I'll get you a blend."

"No, please. If anything, get me one that's a hundred percent cotton. And a size large will do."

"I don't think he has cotton. All his shirts come from Formosa."

"They have cotton in Formosa or import it."

"They might but not in my friend's place. A blend will be okay. They wear well, don't wrinkle that much, and dry in half the time as an all-cotton."

"A blend then. Now what can I do for you?"

"You remember that big storm the other day. Well since then my television reception's been lousy, all sleet and snow, so I think my antenna must have blown down."

"I'll check it on the roof tomorrow."

"You're really a help. If it's not the antenna and you don't think it's anything with the tubes, maybe you can bring it to the repair shop."

I go upstairs. Mr. Bricker calls the next morning. "I just spoke to my friend and he says he has no blends either, so I ordered a large for you in the one you had. You said it was a good-looking shirt and I'm sure after awhile you'll get used to the synthetic material on your back. He said if you wash it real hard a number of times it'll get as smooth as any cotton blend."

"Thank you, Mr. Bricker."

"What? For all the favors you do me, I should be the one to thank you. In fact that's what I'm doing by giving you this shirt—thanking you. So thanks, Michael. Thanks very much."

THE HOLE

The City Planetarium blew up. I was sitting across the street on a park bench at the time. The blast shook the area so hard that my tie and newspaper flew in my face. When I peeled them away I saw pieces of the planetarium's gilded dome dropping around me and flames shooting out of the now domeless theater, in seconds disintegrating the upper branches of the city's oldest and tallest trees.

A woman ran across the street from Planetarium Square. "Two men," she said. "I saw them myself light the dynamite and drive off in a big car. They wore hats and didn't care who was hurt, who was inside," and she beat on her temples and collapsed into my arms.

I took down her name, address and the information she gave, and tried consoling her. But the tighter I held her and the more comforting words I used, the more hysterically she sobbed.

"Excuse me," I said, "but I'm a policeman. On vacation now, which accounts for my civilian dress. But technically on duty all the time, so I have to get over there to see how I can help," and I sat her on the bench and started to cross the street.

Behind me she yelled "Don't leave—I'm afraid. Your duty is as much to protect me as to help them. Because who knows where those men might strike next. Maybe right here," and she jumped off the bench. "Or even down there," and she jumped off the subway grating and darted into the street. "Or even here, or over here, or right here," and she jumped from the sidewalk to the street to the sidewalk again before she ran screaming into the park.

The fire in the planetarium theater had leveled off to a small steady blaze. The building was made of poured concrete, so once the theater seats, carpet and wall paint went up, there wasn't much left to burn but the wood floor.

The planetarium guard told me the children now trapped in the basement cafeteria were having their lunch when the explosion occurred. "For now," he said, "they're probably safe from the fire. Their teacher and two of the kitchen help were with them. And the basement, surrounded by thick sturdy walls, has enough open air ducts to keep them alive. But once the theater floor over them goes and the smoke pours in, then the most useful thing we can do for them is step back from the heat and pray out our hearts for their souls."

The one approachable entrance to the cafeteria was in the lobby through a door completely covered with debris. I flashed my badge to the crowd there and said "Dig. We've all got to dig for those kids," but only the sickly old guard and myself began pulling away the rubble that sealed up the door. I wasn't sure what was keeping the others back. One man said there might be more dynamite behind the door and a woman said she was scared of the young human parts she might find. And there were too many people to cow with the guard's gun as he was urging me to do to get them to help.

The police and fire departments arrived with the best digging, fire-fighting and rescue equipment the city had. In minutes they reached the door leading to the cafeteria and pried it open. Behind it wasn't the empty circular stairway the planetarium director told us to expect, but what looked like a large hole filled to the top with sand, concrete chips and slabs and bits and twists of metal mesh.

"You'll never free them in time," the guard said. "It's too far down— sixteen steps to the cafeteria exact. I know. I've trudged up and down those stairs on my lunch and coffee breaks maybe ten times a day for the past twenty years."

The power-run excavating tools worked rapidly and well till the stair's halfway landing, then became too large and cumbersome when the stairway curved, and the digging stopped.

"Blast the stairway open," a sergeant in Rescue Operations said. He held the explosives, blasting cap and primer cord and was ready to use them the moment the captain gave the command.

"Blast it open," the fire chief said, "and you'll weaken the building's structure entirely, which will cave in the ceiling long before the fire can."

The sergeant said "No offense meant, but I know what I'm talking about also. I've been on more entombments of this kind than I want to recall. Those seven priests buried alive in the Holy Cathedral dynamiting last month, for example. Those forty ballplayers suffocated to death in the locker rooms at the City Stadium bombing last week, for instance."

The captain decided to dig out the trapped people with manual tools. "That way, even if we're unable to rescue them, at least we won't be charged and be saddled with the guilt of having caused the deaths of those children with an unnecessary blast."

There was space for three men in the stairway. I volunteered and was chosen to be part of the second team, which would work when the primary team came up to rest. The one-to-two buddy system of digging was to be used: one man dislodging the embedded slabs while the other men hauled the freed slabs and metal mesh and pails of fragments and earth around the stairway landing to the sling, which when filled would be hoisted out of the hole by a tackle.

The primary team, working on their bellies and knees, dug out the rest of the halfway landing and two of the remaining eight steps to the cafeteria. Then our team went down and was working past a third step when we heard children screaming.

"They're alive," we all yelled, and a roar went off above the ground that I'm sure was loud enough to be heard by the children. We continued to dig and load, the ground beneath us becoming looser and studded with fewer and smaller slabs. After clearing a fourth step I was able to poke a lance to the bottom of the stairs. I flashed a light down the hole and saw three wiggling fingers, then a mustache and mouth.

It was the teacher. He said there were thirty-five children and two elderly female cafeteria employees with him and all were in reasonably good spirits and health. We sent down penlights, chisels and sanitation bags. Then we widened the hole from above while he chipped away at it from below, till the captain came down and said the hole seemed large enough for the smallest of the third-graders to crawl through.

"Make the hole wider so we can all crawl through," the teacher said.

"We'll widen it some more once the kids still down there can't fit through the hole we've already made," the captain said. "That way, we'll at least be sure to get some survivors, as the firemen don't know if they can douse the fire before the ceiling falls."

The teacher said he wouldn't let anyone through till the hole was wide enough for everyone to leave. "I don't see why I should be the one who has the best chance of being left behind in this progressively expanding digging system you've developed, just because I'm by far the largest of my group," and he began widening the hole with the lance and spade we'd sent down and ordering his students and the kitchen ladies to carry the rubble to the other side of the room.

The captain said he didn't think anything would change the teacher's mind right now and ordered the primary team back into the hole.

The primary team dug the hole wide enough for their lead man to squirm through. When he made it to the bottom of the stairs and stuck his head past the mouth of the hole into the cafeteria, the teacher told him to either boost himself back to the top or get a lance in his throat, as he wanted to make sure he could get through the hole himself before he let anyone inside.

The lead man squirmed back up and crawled to the halfway landing with the two haulers. The teacher started to crawl up the stairway hole. But because he was too broad-shouldered when he tried to make it up frontways and big-bottomed when he tried to push himself up hindways, he couldn't get more than a few feet up the hole.

"The hole still needs some widening," he said. "And don't be trying to bully your way down here with any of your thinner police, as my threat to that man before holds true for anyone else barging in. But to encourage you to widen the hole further, and repay you for the good work you've already done, I'm sending up my five smallest students."

Each child emerging from the hole was immediately wrapped in a blanket and carried to the waiting ambulance. None of them seemed sick or in the slightest state of shock. All complained that the blankets were too itchy and warm for them on this hot day, especially after they'd been so long in that hot temperature and stuffiness down there, and what they wanted most was to run around on the cool grass without any shoes or clothes on and breathe fresh air. But they were forcibly held down in the blankets, strapped to the ambulance stretchers and driven to the hospital.

Our team went into the hole again. "How goes it in there?" I asked the teacher, only a few feet from him now and both of us digging away furiously to widen the hole.

He said "Sticky, stifling, nearly suffocating—what do you think?

There's also a little smoke leaking through these ceiling cracks, which means we haven't got long down here if you don't get me out fast."

"Try it now," I said, convinced the hole was wide enough for him. We edged back to the halfway landing as he told us to. He advanced a few feet more than he had the last time, then said he felt as sorry as we must be, but the hole was still too narrow for him to get through.

"Listen," I said. "What'd certainly be worse than dying by yourself in there would be to die with all those kids and kitchen ladies dying around you."

"Listen yourself," he said. "If I know anything about human nature it's that you men will dig a lot harder for me while the kids are down here than if they've all been released. And especially now when you think you know what kind of man you'd be digging out if I happened to end up being stuck alone in here. But I will let the women and some more students up, though not as a digging inducement or rewarding ploy anymore. But because nobody's going to dig a whit harder for two ancient cooking ladies, so I might as well free them to put a stop to their constant nagging and save on the little air we have. And the boys I'm letting out are the ones who always gave me the most trouble in class: puking and bawling now and inciting the rest of my children into an increasingly unmanageable disobedience and maybe a mass physical attack on me soon or total hysteria."

First the cafeteria women came up, looking very frazzled and reviling the police who helped them out of the hole for allowing what they called "that inhuman madman down there" to keep them in that inferno so long. Then seven boys came up. Their faces smudged, bodies limp, hacking and gasping from the smoke in their lungs, all of them fell to the ground when they reached the lobby. One boy yelled to his mother in the crowd. She ducked under the police barrier, clutched her son and screamed into the hole "Butcher . . . murderer . . . you'll get yours quick enough if you ever get up here alive." She fainted and was put on a stretcher alongside the one her son was on, and both were carried to the same ambulance.

"Maybe we better hold up on her," a doctor said, directing the bearers to take her out of the ambulance. "We'll need every stretcher and hospital bed if the kids still down there are suddenly let go."

The woman was lifted off the stretcher and set down on the grass. Several mothers of children still in the cafeteria administered aid to her: holding her hand, massaging her ankles, telling her how lucky she was knowing her son was alive, though she remained unconscious. Her son and the other boys and the cafeteria women were driven to the hospital in a convoy of ambulances and police escorts.

A few hundred people had gathered behind police barriers on the grassy area past the planetarium's driveway. Many of them were calling the police cowards for not forcing their way down the hole to arrest the teacher, and idiots for not shooting him in the hole when they had the chance. The captain said through a bullhorn that any policeman entering the cafeteria wouldn't have had any defense against being lanced as the teacher had sworn to do. "As for shooting him before, an off-target or flesh-exiting bullet could have easily ricocheted into the cafeteria and killed one of the children," but he had to end his explanation because of the jeers from the crowd.

I was sitting on the grass during my rest period when a man standing near me said that today's bombing might wind up producing the city's first lynching in a hundred years. A woman next to him asked if that was a historical fact. "I mean about the possibility of it being the first lynching in a hundred years. I'm a civics professor at the university here, so I'd naturally like to know."

"Two hundred years—even three hundred if you like. What do I know from how long ago the last one was? All I'm saying is it doesn't look like anything could stop this mob from stringing him up. And five gets you the same the police will even be in on it because of the threat to them before. Or at least won't do anything to hold us back—right, officer?" and he patted my back.

I told him that I for one wouldn't take part in any unlawful execution and in fact would do everything in my power to see the teacher got to jail unharmed and order prevailed. The man laughed. The professor said she hoped all the police here felt as I did.

The primary team told the teacher to try the hole again. They moved back to the lobby as he instructed. The teacher crawled to the top of the hole, said "Fine job, very well constructed, we all thank you very much," and returned to the cafeteria and started sending the children up, smallest ones first.

Tired, disheveled, but emotionally calm children were either reunited in the arms of their parents or bundled up in blankets and dispatched to the hospital. Now only the teacher remained. Our team was sent down to assist him or find out what was keeping him from coming up on his own. Near the bottom of the hole we could still hear the parents in the lobby and spectators on the grass screaming for the teacher's neck.

"Will you please halt where you are?" the teacher said from the cafeteria opening, when I told him we wanted to get him out quick as the ceiling was about to cave in. "And no matter how horrible it is for me in here, it sounds as if it'll be worse for me upstairs. But the children and ladies are all right, am I correct in assuming that? Nobody hurt. Everybody alive. A few minor eye and lung ailments which ought to be cleared up in a week. And not only did I preserve the required order down here till everyone was rescued, but my students also learned a vital lesson about life I never could have taught them in class on how to stay alive and deal with their fellow human beings in an emergency situation. Plus an auxiliary lesson related to the city's brotherhood program this week, about how no person should be discriminated against because of his or her age, sex, color, religion, thoughts, health, physiognomy, ethnic, political, geographical or employment group. What I'm ostensibly saying, officer, is that I hope no person or assembly upstairs thinks itself justified in playing jury and executioner with me before I've had my rightful due in the proper courts of law."

"The police will do everything possible to see you get booked and arraigned without incident. Now will you please come along?"

Just then a loud crash came from the cafeteria. Smoke looped around the teacher and up the stairway hole. "That was the ceiling that went," he yelled, "so get, you got to get—I said move."

Our team scurried up the hole into the lobby. Part of the crowd had broken through police lines and were waiting for us at the door, clamoring to kill the teacher the moment he appeared. We thought the teacher was right behind us. But he yelled from the halfway landing that he had decided to stay where he was, lance in hand, till he felt certain his chances for survival were better above ground than below.

"A little gas will get him up," the sergeant in Rescue Operations told the captain, and he loaded a tear gas canister into a gun.

"Force him up before we're sure we can handle this mob," I said, "and we might be delivering him to his killers rather than protecting him from them."

We pushed the crowd back behind the barriers. Many people continued to chant for the teacher's death and threatened to bowl over any police who might try to stop them. The captain told us to let the teacher stay put for the time being. "The mob will have shot its rage and disbanded for their homes and bars in an hour, and then we can get him up without further trouble and over to jail. But if he shows before we tell him it's safe, then all we can conclude is that out of a deep feeling of remorse or something, he intentionally crawled out of the hole to get himself killed."

I was thanked for a job well done and released from emergency duty. I went home and sat for a while at the kitchen table, but wouldn't eat. My mother asked what was disturbing me so much that I couldn't even touch my favorite dinner.

I told her I didn't share the captain's optimism about getting the teacher to jail. "I know something about crowd control and collective violence, and a lot of those people didn't look like they'd leave till they had manipulated the others into helping them lynch him. And this might make me a bad policeman, Mom. But realistically, no healthy sane person wants to get himself killed if he can help it without seriously harming or killing someone else, and that teacher turned out to be the only right one among us after all. Nobody got really hurt or killed. And though I detest his threats against the police, I'm sure we did dig twice as hard because those kids were still with him, which means he would have been buried alive if he'd let them all go all those times we asked him to. And then he wasn't responsible for the bombing or their being entombed. So no matter how evil the mob thinks his motives and methods were, they should at least feel he's gone through enough mishaps and hardships to warrant getting a fair trial."

"Then go back and do what you can for him, since you'll never enjoy your food and vacation the way you are," and I said she was right, phoned the station house and was told the teacher was still in the hole, got my revolver, kept my civies on as I wasn't allowed to be in uniform unless assigned to duty and when going to and from work, and drove to Planetarium Square, hoping the incident would be over by the time I got there and the teacher unharmed and safe in jail.

He was still down there. A crowd a little larger than when I'd left it was still hopping for his neck. The fire was out and the firemen were gone and the captain had been replaced by a lieutenant and most of the police company had been transferred to City Concert Hall across town, as a bomb had exploded there an hour ago and some three hundred people were still trapped in the debris.

I asked the lieutenant if there was anything I could do. He introduced me to the teacher's son and asked if I'd mind accompanying the young man down the hole so he could try to coax his father up. "I don't want him going in alone. He might leave provisions or clothing on the sly or even stay down there himself, making it even tougher getting the teacher up later on. Now's the most opportune time to get him out too. The darkness should conceal his escape movements if we can avoid tipping off the mob with any scuffling or squabbling sounds from below. If we wait till morning I'm afraid the mob will be larger and doubly intent on getting revenge on him for his treatment of his students before and this new rash of bombings and now all those deaths at Concert Hall. But this is a volunteer assignment, you understand. You're still on vacation. I wouldn't order any man to risk facing a lance while on his chest. But since the teacher seemed to trust you most and you know the hole better than anyone else around, you're the most suitable man for the job."

We entered the hole. The son, lagging behind me, complained about his knees being scraped and brand new sandals and slacks getting torn, then apologized for his self-centeredness and said anything was worth ripping and ruining to save his dad. We both carried flashlights and spoke softly as we crawled.

"We're coming, Dad."

"Though please don't make any fuss or objections about it," I said.

"We want you to come out quietly with us for your own good."

"I'm the officer who was the lead man for that back-up digging team."

"He's very sympathetic to you and came with me only to help."

"Your son will confirm that now's the best chance you'll have for ditching that mob upstairs."

"It's true, Dad."

"I'm armed. But to show my good faith, I'll leave the gun behind me anytime you say."

The teacher never answered. We crawled to the end of the stairway without finding him. The ceiling caving in before had blocked the cafeteria entrance again. We checked and rechecked the entire hole with our flashlights till I spotted a tiny aperture in the wall where the stairway curved. We broke through the wall, enlarged the opening wide enough to fit through. Behind it was an empty basement corridor still lit by electric lights and seemingly untouched by the explosion and fire. It was about thirty feet long and had a door at either end of it.

I opened one door and found nothing behind it but soap powder and cleaning equipment. The son ran and stood in front of the other door. "Come on," he said. "What's the harm if we let him get out on his own?"

"The harm's that I was sent down to get him up safely, not let him escape."

"He'll be escaping from the mob, not the police. He'll turn himself in tomorrow when he's sure it's safe enough. I know my old man. He's extremely legal-conscious, has an unflagging respect for the law. He'll want to face up to all the charges brought against him, and if guilty, he'll gladly serve his time."

"I promise to do everything I can to see he gets to court. Now will you please let me get on with my job?" I pushed him aside, opened the door and found the room or passageway behind it packed with rubble. We searched the corridor and utility closet for an exit the teacher might have gone through, but there were no other doors, vents or tiny holes.

"He couldn't have just vanished," I said.

"What are we going to tell them upstairs?"

"That he couldn't have just vanished."

"They'll never believe us. Both the mob and police will say we were in on the escape. And the longer we stay down here, the less they'll believe he got away on his own. We have to think up some airtight excuse right away. What about that he fell down a shaft made by the bombing before and which then crumbled apart and buried him?"

"And if he turns up tomorrow as you say?"

"Maybe his great respect for the law and its court system has finally wavered."

"No. The lieutenant will send some men down to try and dig him out."

"Then what about that he took your gun and made us dig through the cafeteria entrance and got out some way through there?"

"No. They'll want to know why we filled in the hole after him."

"So we did it at gunpoint or he filled it up himself."

"Then they'll want to know why I still have my gun on me."

"We'll say he threw it back just before he put the last stone in the hole."

"No. They'll dig through the cafeteria entrance and probably find there isn't another escape route through there."

"How do we know? Maybe there is. But the reason he couldn't find it before is because for most of his time in the cafeteria he had no light."

"The kitchen ladies would have told him of another exit when they were with him."

"Then a new hole or old sealed one they didn't know about could have been opened by the explosion."

"It's too far-fetched."

"It'll get us off the hook for now. What about that he went through that second corridor door when he saw us breaking through the wall, and which immediately caved in behind him just as he got past?"

"The lieutenant will get the floor plans. And that door might lead to nothing but a storage room and freezer locker and lavatory and another utility closet with no other way out of these rooms but the doors leading to the room with the door to the corridor that he came through."

"Then what about that he fell down a shaft made by the bombing before and which then crumbled apart and buried him?"

We gave up trying to find a plausible excuse and returned to the lobby and told the lieutenant the truth.

"No chance," he said. He sent several men into the hole to find the teacher or the exit he used. "And this time," he yelled down the stairway to the men, "shoot to disable if he won't come up nice and sweetlike by himself. We're through pussyfooting around that guy just to prevent the unlikely prospect of his getting beaten up or lynched."

The men came up an hour later saying they discovered a chute in the utility closet that led down to a small room that had nothing in it but dirty table linen and uniforms and a door plugged up with impassable debris. Other men were sent down to look for possible escape routes in the laundry room and chute, utility closet, corridor and stairway hole, but all they could come up with were two six-inch across air ducts filled with concrete chips and sand.

"How are we going to explain this to the mob?" I asked the lieutenant.

"Very simply that he got away through an opening we've yet to uncover."

"Think they'll believe that?"

"What do I care what they believe? As long as they can mull it over for a while and I get them off my back."

"But they'll say we're still holding him till they leave."

"Then we'll let a few crowd representatives into the hole to inspect the stairway and laundry room."

"When they don't find him they'll say we knowingly let him go to avert disorder."

"So we'll tell them we smuggled the teacher through the lobby as we'd first planned to, and he's now in a downtown jail."

"They'll find out later tonight or tomorrow we don't have him. And when the papers get wind of it we'll be in even worse trouble with a bigger mob, with the jail liable to get destroyed."

"Then we'll tell them exactly what happened, because we haven't any more time to think up an excuse. There was a bombing at City Art Museum a half hour ago and we're all needed there to dig out the night guards and works of art."

He ordered his men into the police vans. Two policemen were kept behind to guard the stairway, just in case the teacher had been hiding some place in the hole all this time and was waiting to leave through the lobby after everyone had gone. I was asked to make sure the son got home all right and then to resume what the lieutenant called my much-interfered-with-though-more-than-ever-now-well-earned vacation.

He addressed the crowd, told them of the most recent bombing and of his new assignment and that the teacher had apparently given the police the slip. "Though nobody should worry any about it, as we've excellent photos and fingerprints of the man, so it won't be more than a day or two before he's caught. So break it up, everybody. We don't want total chaos and terror becoming the rule of our city. Go back to your homes or jobs or to a quiet bar if you can find one, as there's just no sensible reason left to stick around," and satisfied the crowd was splitting up and leaving, he and his unit drove to the museum.

The crowd quickly re-formed. A group of men bulldozed its way past the two policemen and went into the hole. The son and I stood in the dark behind a parked car nearby in case the teacher was turned up. The group came out and said they'd found nothing new downstairs but a trapdoor in the laundry chute that tunneled through to a sewer pipe that wasn't wide enough to fit a kitten in.

The son and I crossed the street and were hailing a cab coming out of the park when a woman shouted "Why are we letting the cop get off free? Wasn't he the one who was so chummy with the teacher, and for all we know came back here to sneak him past us and the police?"

"That's not quite true," I said, when the crowd began forming around us and the cab. "I'll admit I did come back here to see what I could do to get him past you all and safe in jail, but I had no specific plan as to how I'd bring it off. And I only went into the hole a second time because the lieutenant felt the best way to get the teacher to jail without any police and civilians getting hurt was for the teacher's son and I to quietly coax him up into a police van, though we never saw a trace of him."

"His son?" a man said. "Then he's the one we ought to be getting. He's got the same kind of blood in his veins, so he'll be doing the same thing to our kids his dad did if he ever gets the chance. We'll be doing a favor to a whole slew of people in the future by doing away with him now."

The son bolted through the crowd. I yelled "Don't run, you fool, you'll only provoke them more." The cab drove off with its back doors flapping and people pounding its sides with sticks. Some men chased after the son. I drew my revolver, was grabbed from behind, knocked to the ground and sat on while part of the crowd disarmed the policemen who tried to help me. They caught the son, dragged him back, kicked at his head and body till it seemed all his limbs, ribs and face were broken, then hung him upside down by his feet from one of the tree branches that had survived the fire. They continued to spit at him and some women pulled out patches of his hair and beat his already unrecognizable face with their handbags, till one of the policemen said "All right, folks. I think you did everything you could do to him short of setting him on fire, so why don't you go home." Someone lit a match to the son's shirtsleeve, but the policemen slapped the fire out.

The crowd broke up. One of the men who'd been sitting on me said "Just thank your lucky stars you told us the truth." Some people as they walked away from the square turned around every few seconds to give the body dirty looks.

I cut the rope holding the son: he came down on his head. The policemen put him in a canvas sack and that sack into the trunk of their squad car. No charges were brought against anyone for the son's death. The following day the newspapers said the son had died from a fall inside the stairway hole while looking for his father, who was still being sought by the police. The police, the articles said, were still trying to determine the causes and persons responsible for the planetarium bombing and other related explosions. So far they've had no success.

JOKE

She takes off my shoes, gets up, goes to the kitchen with the shoes, comes back, sits next to me, takes off my pants, gets up, goes to the bathroom with the pants, comes back, sits beside me, takes off my jacket, gets up, I say "Where you going this time?" she says nothing, leaves with my jacket, I don't know where she is, comes back, looks the same, no more makeup than before, she hasn't taken anything off or put anything on herself or changed her hair style since I got here, sits beside me, takes off my socks, gets up, I say "What now?" she says "I've got to go," I say "Where?" she says "You know where," I say "No, where is 'you know where'—where I'm supposed to think it is, wherever that is, or someplace else?" she says "Maybe" and goes, I say "Damn, I'm getting tired of all your getting up and going and coming back and sitting and then going again," but she doesn't answer, maybe she didn't hear me, just like before she comes back in two minutes and sits beside me, takes off my shirt, gets up, I grab her hand, she says "Let go," I say "But where you off to this time if I can ask?" she says "None of your business," I say "You don't think it's partly my business or at least that I should think it odd your repeatedly taking off something of mine and disappearing with it right after and not bringing it back?" and she says "Let go of my hand first," I let go, she goes, down the hall again which could be to any number of places: the two bedrooms, the bank of closets, the front door, out of it or standing near it, the stairway outside the front door, the other apartment on the floor, the flight up to the roof or the four flights down to the ground floor or street, though probably not out there and back in two minutes unless she ran all the way, though I didn't hear the front door open or close and she wasn't breathing hard when she returned, though the door could have been open from one of the two previous times she went down the hall with my clothes when I wasn't listening as closely as I did this time and she could be in even better shape than I thought, anyway she's back, two minutes, no change, shirt gone, sits beside me, takes off my underpants, "Now I'm naked," I say, "Except for your cap," she says, "Oh I always leave my cap on,"

"No, this time I won't let you leave it on," "Yes I say," "No I say," "All right," I say, "take it off," "Later," she says and gets up, I grab her wrist, "I swear you're making me mad no matter how nice our conversation just was," "Tough," she says, "Don't make me even madder," I say, "Tough," she says, "You're making me much madder, Dotty," "Tough tough tough," she says and jerks her wrist out of my hand and goes down the hall with my underpants to any of the places I mentioned before, or maybe to none of them, maybe she's just staying out of sight from me in the hall to make me madder than I am, or maybe she did leave the front door open from any of those last times she went down the hall and now goes out to do something or see someone in any of the stairways or other apartments or vestibules, roof, another building or street, but she comes back, two minutes, "Where you been?" I say, sits beside me, "What are you going to take off me now?" I say, knocks off my cap, "Now there's nothing to take off me," gets up, "I'm not going to stop you this time," I say, leaves the room with my cap, "You want to know why I didn't stop you?" she's somewhere in the hall or any of the other places or one I haven't thought of yet, "Because I want to see what you're going to take off me next," comes back, I say "Well hello there, Dotty," sits beside me, "What you got planned for me now, Dotty?" puts her lips near my mouth, "That a way to go there, friend Dotty," kisses me and leaves a blob of something on my tongue, I take it out, "What did you do that for, this old prune which for all I know was in your filthy pocket first," takes it out of my hand, "Oh, still undressing me, Dotty, that's what your prune's supposed to signify?" starts down the hall with it, "Oh, going to deposit it with my other things you took down that way?" comes back, in about two minutes, "What are you going to stick in my mouth this time?" I say, sits beside me, "I'm curious, for this is quite the game you're playing—more prunes, a wad of gum? Well, I'm not kissing you if it seems like it's going to be anything like that," she just looks at my eyes, "Maybe something else you're going to stick in or on me this time so you can take it out or off me, right?" still just looking at me, "Well, I'm not going to let you even touch me till you're totally undressed yourself," just looking at me, "Then it is all right, if you're through undressing me, if I start taking off your clothes?" blank expression, eyes blinking naturally but never looking away from mine, "Then how about if I start undressing you without your permission?" still just looking at me, "Okay, I'm going to do it, now I warned you, Dotty" and I slip off one of her shoes. She kicks my hand. I start removing the other shoe. She punches my jaw. I slap her face. She pulls my hair. I swat her with my open hand. She pulls me up and knees me in the groin. I fall over. She pounds my head with the shoe I took off her. She pounds it a lot. She pounds it before I can stop her pounding it some more. She pounds and pounds it. I'm on the ground on my face. I try but can't get up. She's still pounding my head. "I didn't know," I say, maybe to myself when I want to say it aloud, "I didn't know this all wasn't to you mostly a joke."

THE GOLD CAR

She drives up in a gold car. A crowd's in front of the house. She saw the crowd when she turned the corner. At first she thought the crowd was in front of his house or the houses on either side of it. As she got closer she knew it was in front of his. There was very little overlapping of the crowd on the lawns of the houses next to his. Groups have been in front of his house before. Either just to look at it and take photographs, just because he lives there, or to get his autograph by waiting for him in front of the house or by walking up to the door and ringing the bell. But this crowd was about three times as large as any she'd seen in front of his house, and she now sees a policewoman in it. She gets out of the car, takes off her sunglasses, puts on her prescription glasses, gets her shoulder bag and walks up the path to the house. "What is it?" she says to the first person she comes to. Several people turn to her and say "Sid Anscott died."

It was early morning when she left, she tells the policeman. "What time early?" he says. "Ten, ten-fifteen. I went to get some milk and eggs and things—fresh breads, rolls and bagels if they had any. Sid loved bagels or rolls for breakfast. I haven't known him for long so I wasn't too familiar with his neighborhood. But he was all out of everything and I thought I'd do him a favor for once. Oh, I've done him lots of favors, but you know what I mean: going out and surprising him by getting breakfast food while he slept. But I met an old friend at the market—Lucille Booth—and she said 'Let's have a coffee, I haven't seen you for months.' So I went to a coffee shop with her but called Sid at home. No answer. I knew he'd be up by now, so I thought he was either in the shower or had gone out for a run. He was overweight, as you probably know, but liked to run every single morning."

Sid was sleeping when she got out of bed. She didn't think he was breathing right and she shook him a little. "Sid, Sid," she said. He said "What?" She said "You're not sleeping right—you're breathing so hard. Anything wrong?" "No," he said. "I'm sorry for waking you then,

130

I was just worried." He said "Leave me alone, will you—let me sleep."
He never moved his head or opened his eyes when he said all this. She
said "Sorry, honey, I'm really sorry—just go back to sleep." She went
to the bathroom, doing stretching exercises as she went. She washed up,
then went into the kitchen and opened the refrigerator. She felt like having a glass of some kind of cold juice, orange most of all. The refrigerator
and its freezer were empty except for a bottle of champagne on its side,
two six-packs of beer, butter, wilted vegetables, hamburger meat and
rolls. No juice, milk, nothing like that. She'd get some juice and other
things, she thought. She went back to the bedroom. He was still asleep.
She said, "Sid, Sid, mind if I borrow the car to get some groceries—
you're all out." He said something but she wasn't sure if it was "Go
ahead" or "Let me sleep." Anyway, she knew he wouldn't mind if she
took the car. She'd done it a few times before and the last time without
asking him. She got the car keys off the dresser and thought about taking
some money out of his wallet, but didn't. She had enough of her own
and what the hell, he'd been plenty generous with her last night, taking
her to an expensive restaurant and before that to a bar where they had
these great Hawaiian cocktails that must have cost five dollars each. Of
course he could afford it, but she knew he'd appreciate her thinking of
him as someone who didn't have to pick up the tab every time. Then she
got dressed and drove to the market where, when she was paying for the
groceries, she met Lucille.

"So tell me what you've been up to lately?" Lucille said in the coffee
shop. "Let me phone Sid again—I don't want him to worry." "Sid
who?" Lucille said. "Sid Anscott—but don't tell anyone. His wife's not
supposed to know, nor, to tell you the truth, his agent, who's a good
friend of his wife." "Oh I won't, sweetie, I won't. But good for you. He's
very big now, very very big. Does he treat you right?" "Why shouldn't
he?" "He has a reputation of not treating his women right, his wife fore-
most among them." "That's out of the magazines and ugly gossip papers. He's a doll. He's beautiful. I love him. He's sweet as cake." "Okay,
all right, you convinced me. From now on someone asks what kind of
guy he is, I'll say better than Christ and more romantic, though I won't
say where I heard it from. And love, is it?" "I said so, not that I expect

anything from it. He said he'd never get divorced. He's very honest about it. He tells me staying married keeps him from making the same mistake twice. I go along with it. It lasts a month more, fine; a year, better. But he says I'm special and it could go on for he doesn't know how long, and I believe him. Why shouldn't I? He treats me like I should believe him." "So, to answer my question finally," Lucille said, "he does treat you well, right?" "He got me on the payroll of his new movie. Not in acting but working with the script. Technical things, and on location. It's terrific experience. It might even get me better jobs in that line, and if it does, then the hell with acting. I'm sick of it already and it's got me almost nothing so far but a date with him which led to the script job and possibly better things after. Sure, better things after. But it's enough that I'm with him, without the job or anything, though it's certainly better with the job." "He sounds okay," Lucille said, "— much better than what I've heard of him. Maybe he's changed or maybe everyone else was wrong." "I got to go to the phone."

His phone rang. Screw it, who's calling so early? he thought. The phone continued to ring. "Bea, get the phone, will you?" he said, "I'm still too freaking bushed." The phone continued to ring and then stopped. He felt for her on the bed. He turned over. Where the hell is she? "Bea," he yelled, "hey Bea." Oh yeah, that's right, took the car, went for groceries. Good girl; I'm hungry already. He got up. Who the hell was that on the phone anyway? Doesn't everybody who knows my number know I'm not to be disturbed till twelve? Well what do you know, looking at the clock. Ten after. So someone for once was paying attention. He went into the bathroom. Oh mama, what a head. He got two aspirins out of the jar—make it three, you're a big fella—too freaking big, squeezing his belly, and ran the water awhile before he filled up a glass, let the cloud in it disappear and drank the water down. Best way to avoid ulcers from aspirins, the water, and to avoid burping from those clouds.

"Officer, this woman seems to know Mr. Anscott." She was being held up by two men. "Someone—say, someone," the policewoman said, "bring out a chair. No, inside bring her. Bring her inside. Here, I'll take over. Bram," she called to a policeman at the door, "give me a hand." The two officers brought her into the house. She was crying. She said "They said he's dead. I just left him a few hours ago, how could he be dead? I left him in bed sleeping." "You're his wife, ma'am?" Bram said. "No, his wife is in New York." "You're a good friend then—a business associate?" "Sure, both, but you want to know, it'll come out anyhow. I'm a very good friend. We've been together for more than a month now. I have my own place but last night I stayed here with him. You'll find some of my clothes in his closet and some of my evening clothes over the chair in the bedroom. Could you please tell me what happened?" "You sure you don't want a lawyer first?" the policewoman said. "We want you to know all your rights." "What do I need a lawyer for? They said he died and your looks aren't denying it. I was outside at the time. I went to the market for us. I'm absolutely heartsick at the whole thing. What do I need a lawyer for? My problem is nothing except that he's dead. What could he have died of, could you please tell me?" "Look," the policewoman said, "why don't you sit down? Yes, that's a good idea. Bram, will you get her some water, and then you can tell us what happened right from the time you last saw him here. When was that exactly and what's your full name?"

She put the key into the ignition. Boy, she thought, wouldn't it be great to own a car like this, and if she still lived where she lives, to have the money to garage it. She drove off. Let's see: eggs, milk, bread, rolls, bagels if they have, orange juice, muffins even, butter because the butter he has is probably rancid, pancake mix. Did he have pancake mix? Should've checked. But the heck with pancake mix. He said he wants to lose weight. His studio in fact insists he lose weight and I'm now working for the studio. So what do you buy for breakfast and lunch—a brunch—for a man who will wake up starved after so long a sleep and when he really didn't eat that much the night before, expensive as the food was, but who wants to lose weight? Grapefruit. The biggest pinkest grapefruit they have. Two of them. And maybe cottage cheese and plain yogurt and a jar of dietary marmalade. I know he loves it because when we went to that chalet in Arizona he practically ate the whole cup of marmalade they gave us. And maybe for his coffee I'll warm the skim milk it's going to be and serve him breakfast in bed. No, that would be too corny. A car pulled up alongside hers when she was waiting for the light to change. Oh, the dapper type—a ladykiller. Bushy mustache, shirt unbuttoned to the navel, car looking like it was polished just today. Look at the way he combs his hair. Must've taken him an hour to get it set that way. Nice looking though. He's going to say something. I know it's going to come. Here it is, folks. "A very fine-looking automobile," he said through her passenger window, "and a very attractive driver handling it as well. That's all I have to say. If you want to talk more I'll be parked on the right side just beyond the next traffic light." The light changed and he took off before her. What a character. I wonder how many women he picks up a month with that line. In this town, with those looks and that car, I bet he does all right. It's sad though—just depressing, to think that that's what relationships have come to. What do I mean by that? That it's just in and out, meet me at the light, do it in the hotel, see you, sweetface, without most times either person catching the other's name. Actually, things longer lasting can come from pickups like that. Didn't I meet Sid at that screening in almost a similar way? I'm at the refreshment stand wondering what to buy for the movie when he comes over to buy something too, or so he said, but I'm sure with his appetite it was true, and he said "Hey, you think if we buy two boxes of popcorn at the same time they'll give us a break on the price?" I said I didn't know. I immediately recognized him. He said "What about one giant pail between us, no break on the price, but we have to sit next to each other to eat it?" I'm game, I said. So we ordered a giant pail. I insisted on paying for it—after all, I told him, "you don't look like you can afford it." He got a big laugh out of that. We went home after a late evening snack together—his home, in this car, since he wanted me to leave mine in the parking lot rather than follow him in it, and he'd drive me to it the next morning. So we slept together that night and here we are, a month later, with me minus my car because of that night, but that turned out all right thanks to Sid, and us much closer than we ever were and I think getting closer all the time. She drove past the next light—it was green—and there sure enough was that guy from before. She waved to him as she passed. He honked his horn and pulled out and at the next street made a right.

Sally rang the doorbell of Sid's house. There was no answer. She rang again and again. What in God's name is wrong with him? You make appointments, you keep them. She rang some more, then tried the door. Locked. Well, why shouldn't it be in any neighborhood in this city, and if it was open what did she think she'd do, go in? Maybe. She'd at least open the door a little and say into the house "Sid? It's Sally. You said you wanted me to come by at noon, so here I am. I brought the publicity photos and blurbs. All you have to do is look them over and check which ones you like." Well, she wouldn't say all that. Just "Sid, it's Sally, you there?" Maybe he's in the back of the house or having his coffee on the patio. She went through the gate, didn't even see a chair out there, and knocked on the rear door. No answer. He did say one time when she came here and he didn't answer though he was home that if it happened again, just go around the house and walk in. "You see me naked," he said, "scream, but don't rip your clothes off right away, as I might be with my wife." "Oh, funny guy, this Sid," she said, "funny, funny. We're strictly business, for now and forever, got that straight?" "Straight, yes, you said it, baby, I didn't—because if I can avoid it I wouldn't do it any other way. But only kidding. I've more than my share of complications already, so why kill the hen that gave the golden goose, hey?" She said "I'm hardly the golden goose—I might work for a few who aren't so golden—so maybe at the most I'm a three-minute soft-boiled egg." He said "Good, great, write that down for me—I call you a hen, you call yourself an egg. Beautiful, what a yak; I'm going to use it next time I want to lay one." She knocked on the rear door again and opened it slightly. "Sid, it's Sally, you around? Hello? Nobody home?" He could be in the shower or sauna. She went into the house and called "Sid? Sid?" as she walked through it. "Anybody else around? One of Sid's friends?" The bathroom door was open. She went in and knocked on the sauna, but the red light was off so she knew no one was inside. She went into the kitchen, then to the bedroom. The door was open, room was dark, blinds were closed. She saw him on the floor naked, and beside him part of a hamburger roll.

Herman gets a phone call from Fritz who tells him Sid Anscott died this morning. "Probably of natural causes. Got some food lodged in his windpipe and choked to death. But that's just the on-the-scene report—he's now with the coroner. Want me to make a statement for us to the press?" "Do what you feel comfortable with," Herman says, "but be nothing but straight-out flattering. We loved, unbelievable loss, he was the greatest—that sort of stuff. But before you say anything to anybody, get hold of his wife and tell her if she doesn't know—I can't," and hangs up. Poor Sid, he thinks. And the poor studio. And the studio's even poorer insurance company if it pays up. And the poor girl he was seeing now and he asked me to put on the payroll. And his poor wife though she won't be so poor in other ways once his estate's settled. And his own poor kid and his poor mother. And all the poor kids and mothers and grandmothers who are going to be pouring their eyes out once they hear about Sid. This calls for a meeting. For how in the world are we going to finish three-quarters of a picture without him? Later. I got a few days to decide. Now I just feel too bad. He presses a button on the telephone, puts the receiver down and goes into the next room. "Willie," he says to his secretary, "get me Fritz again. I want to ask if anyone's thought about the funeral arrangements. No, I don't want to speak to anyone for ten minutes, so tell him from me, please, that the quicker we get Sid back and buried, the less time they'll have to see what a mess he made of his body. But not to lean, tell him, on the police or medical examiner, because then they might dig even deeper into that poor guy."

Fritz calls Sid's wife in New York a third time and Sid's daughter says "I told you, my mother's at a class now and won't be home till six." "It's not six now?" Fritz says. "I'm sorry, honey, I always get those California-New York time differences mixed up. But your mother comes in before six, give her the number I gave you and my name, okay?" What should I do? he thinks after he hangs up. Call up again and break it to the kid before she hears it on the radio? Because it's going to be on the radio soon or in their late edition paper. It might even be on it now. He calls Herman and says "One or the other of us has to tell Sid's kid if we can't get his wife in the next half hour. The kid will be shocked even worse out of her wits if she first hears it on the radio or TV. Worse on TV if they have a picture of Sid, and much worse if they have one of him on the floor." "I'll do it," Herman says, "but how old you think that girl is?" "Fifteen, sixteen, by her voice." "Ten," Herman says, "if that. But so grown up. Too grown up for even a sixteen year old, but that's what to expect, I guess, for those California kids with successful showbiz parents, even if they live in New York. I used to hold that little angel on my knees and she once took a swing at me—innocently, I mean—and broke my glasses. Ah, maybe you should call Jenkins and have him rush over to their apartment instead."

Sausages, she thought. Why not link sausages and eggs? She'll poach the eggs even if he doesn't have a poacher. She knows how. Water boiling—frying pan, she'll have to use—drop the eggs in just right with a spoon, curl them over and cover and three to four minutes they're done. That'll at least make up for the grease and extra calories in the sausages. Or bacon. How about that? Not the most original idea, but broiled almost to a crisp in the stove and then stretched out on a paper towel and delicately patted till the bacon's dry. She wishes they had spackle in L.A. They have everything else including better bagels than even in Brooklyn, Sid's said—"It took people like me to insist they make them better if they want to keep a colony of New Yorkers here"—and cheese better than maybe even in Italy and France and certainly as good as wines as they got there—but what's she going on about? She doesn't want wine for brunch but something very sobering after last night—coffee, the richer the better. So some dark espresso coffee to mix in with the regular coffee too. He even have any regular coffee in the house? She doesn't remember seeing it, so get a pound can of regular coffee and a half pound of espresso and maybe even croissants if they have no bagels or good rolls. No, too fattening. He'll complain about it to me after he eats every one. So just sausages or bacon, eggs, a tomato or two, grapefruit, a little low-fat solid cheese, but not yellow—too many chemicals in that one, he's said—and the coffees and yogurt and cottage cheese and that should do it. Milk and orange juice, of course. It'll be a great breakfast. And butter.

When they got back to the parking lot the next day, her car had been stolen. Sid yelled at the parking lot attendant "Didn't you have someone here all night?" "Easy, babe," the attendant said. "At midnight, it says on the sign there, the lot's closed and unattended, so the car owners keep it here at their own risk. Read it, babe. I hope your buggy was insured." "Was it?" Sid asked Bea. "I don't think so for theft," she said. "It was my sister's." "Well if it wasn't insured I'll pay your sis back whatever she would've got for it if it had been insured—bluebook value, and she can also rent one on me till the insurance comes through. It wasn't a new one, was it? Eh, what's the difference? Let's look at it positively: from now on you'll have to be dependent on me." "Maybe first thing we should do is call the police." "You're a genius. I'll drive you there and wait outside, as I don't want to get involved if you can understand." He gave the attendant a twenty-dollar bill. For what? To keep his mouth shut, she supposed, for after the attendant and he had that little argument, the attendant said "Say, babe, aren't you Sid Anscott? I knew I recognized you, but in that hat and glasses and all, you fooled me a second. Those lenses for real?"

Sid's wife sits in the classroom listening to the lecture. What ever made him think he was interesting enough to listen to and with that squeaky voice, and me think I could go back to school after hating it all my life? "Plague, and the death of Pericles in four twenty-nine—that's B.C., *B.C.*—severely lowered Athenian morale," the teacher says. Someone knocks on the door. The whole class looks over to it and the teacher says "If that's anyone late again—yes? enter," after someone knocks again. The door opens. Her daughter and Jack Jenkins come in. Something's very wrong, she thinks. I bet Sid got into a car accident and died. She stands up. "Mommy," Sonya says and runs over to her and grabs her around the waist and presses her head to her breast. "Excuse me," the teacher says, "but what is going on?" Jenkins says to the teacher, while Margo's asking him "What is it, Jack, what's wrong?" "It's all right, sir, sorry for this little disturbance," and takes her arm as he rubs Sonya's shoulder and says "I've something dreadful to tell you, Margo, just the worst thing possible. I think we should step outside." "Daddy's dead," Sonya says.

The bag of groceries was beside her when she drove back to Sid's house. He's going to love what I got for him, she thought. She saw a jogger running past her going the opposite way and thought it's not beyond the realm of possibility that Sid might be jogging along here too. Twice before he was when she was driving back and both times she stopped and said something like "Like a lift, gorgeous?" He said no, but rather matter-of-factly—he was a serious jogger despite his being overweight and that he didn't jog more than two miles a day—"I better run the rest of the way home." The first time he said that, she said "If I drive you home I'll get into my sneakers and shorts and run with you for a mile." "No really," he said, "I don't like to stop. All I want now is to finish my run, take a shower and have a big fat glass of water. See you," and he started to run. The second time she only said when he said he wanted to continue his run, "Whoops, forgot; see you at home," and drove off. Now she saw another man running in her direction from about a block away. Looks like Sid, she thought. Same red T-shirt. The shorts though—blue? He doesn't have blue shorts far as she knows. She got nearer and saw the runner was too thin to be Sid. Then she turned the corner and saw a crowd in front of his house or the houses on either side of his.

THE NEW JOB

I put down the newspaper. Lynn says "What's in the papers?"

I tell her: foreign crisis this, domestic situation that. She says "Doesn't sound as if it was worth reading."

"Gave me something to do," I say.

"Maybe you ought to try something else, like not reading the papers."

"For instance?"

"For instance finding something that might earn you some money."

"I looked Monday through Thursday all day for work and couldn't find anything, so today I'm taking off. I just thought I needed a rest."

"A rest from not working?"

"A rest from looking."

"Today if you looked might've been the day you found work."

"I thought one day off from looking would give me the I-don't-know-what. Luck, that's what. Friday's the worst day for finding work anyway and Monday I think I'll really get a job."

"What makes you so sure?"

"I'm not. I just think I will. I feel it. No, I don't even think or feel it. I probably won't find work. I probably never will. That the attitude you want me to have? Well I now have it. I don't know, Lynn. I was feeling good about finding work Monday till a couple minutes ago when we started this talk. Excuse me, no offense meant by my leaving the room," and I get up, leave the room, don't know where I'm going but in this small apartment there aren't many places I can go and I end up in the kitchen. What can I do here? No place to sit, just a little moving around space. I open the refrigerator. Nothing good inside. Baloney, piece of cream cheese, eggs, vegetables, milk and fruit, most a few days old and not fresh, but all bought with what she earns from her job. Coffee. Make some coffee. Coffee usually does the trick and it'll give me something to do. Or walk. Day's okay. Take a long walk. But do something. What I'd like to do most is nap. But she'd be on me. "Sure," she'd say, "go ahead. Sleep all day. Right through the evening too when I'm waiting on tables

140

and running around till my feet are falling off. Sleep all day if you want. Don't forget to drink all day also. And run after women all day too. All that. Go on."

Maybe she wouldn't say that. Maybe she'd understand.

I go into the living room. "Lynn, I've something to tell you."

"You want a divorce."

"Don't be silly."

"Oh, that's too bad."

"What do you mean?"

"Nothing."

"You had to mean something. You talk about divorce as though you're the one who wants one. Do you?"

"Of course not."

"Why'd you bring it up then?"

"What did you have to tell me?"

"First tell me why you brought up the subject of divorce?"

"I was just talking. Joking. I was totally unserious. I just thought, when I saw your serious face come in the room, that you had something very serious to tell me, so I took the most serious thing I could think of and said it. I didn't think it was divorce you wanted to talk to me about but something else serious, that's all I meant by my remark. Now what was it?"

"I wanted to know if . . . no, forget it."

"Come on, don't make me drag it out of you. Say it. What? I can take anything. I'm no longer mad or whatever I was at you before."

"Mad."

"Well I'm no longer. I know you've looked hard for work. I also know you need a rest from looking so hard for work. So really, go on, rest, sit and read the papers if you want all day. Do anything you want like that. Okay?"

"You mean that?"

"Mean it."

"Because you know I don't like being unemployed and depending on you for all our money."

"I know. You were never a goof-off ever. It's just bad times, that's all."

"For lots of people."

"I know. But it'll get better for you. I don't know about the other peo-ple. They might mostly be slouches, but you're not. You'll find what you're looking for though you got to know beforehand what that is and also what not to look for."

"I'm looking for work in my old field, what else is there to look for?"

"But you know it's impossible getting work there. That field has just about dried up. I didn't want to say it again because I don't like repeat-ing myself and I know what I say about this makes you mad, but maybe you should start looking for work in some new undried-up field."

"Like what?"

"Like whatever you're good at."

"I'm only good at doing what I did in the old . . . oh, the hell, forget it. I'll never find work. Every time I talk to you about it I eventually get depressed. Forget what I was going to tell you. I'm just going to do it. I'm going to bed."

"That's what you wanted to tell me?"

"Yes. I was going to say I'm tired and depressed and I just want to go to bed in the middle of the day and sleep for maybe forty-eight hours straight if that's what I need to come out of my depression and tiredness refreshed. And that I don't want you harping on me if you saw me going to bed at this time of the day. But I don't care now if you harp on me. I'm going to bed. I have to. I have to go to sleep. I have to forget what time of the day it is and that some people are working this time of the day and I'm not and might never be and that I haven't worked for six months and that I'm depressed as hell because of all this and also because you're pay-ing all the bills and are secretly and sometimes outwardly angry at me for not having a job in six months and so on. So I'm going to bed. Good night. I mean, good day or whatever one says to someone when he goes to bed at midday. But that's what I'm doing."

I head for the bedroom.

"You say to someone in that case," she says, "that 'I'm a goof-off and I feel sorry for myself without bounds and I'm maybe going crazy and maybe becoming a baby again because only a baby goes to bed at mid-day or a real worker who deserves to because he's worked the early morning shift.' That's what you should say. That you're getting worse and worse. That you maybe need a psychiatrist."

"If I need one, then I should go to one. But to go to one I need money and certainly you won't give me any for one. But maybe I need a drink too," and I turn from the bedroom door and go to the kitchen and get the wine jug out of the cabinet and pour a glass of wine.

She comes in. "Drinking too. My prediction before's come true. Why not bring women home like I also said and sleep with them here too? Why not run naked in the street? Goddammit, why not kill yourself too?"

I go into the bedroom with my wine and take off my clothes and sit naked on the bed and drink some of the wine and open the book I left on the night table last night and read. She comes in.

"I'm sorry," she says. "I apologize completely, really. I didn't mean for you to go kill yourself at all. I didn't mean to bring up other women or to criticize you for drinking a single glass of wine before you take a two-day nap or whatever today. I'm just feeling lousy. Because you're depressed, I'm depressed. Which only probably makes you even more depressed, my getting depressed. I know you've looked hard for work. I've said that, but I also know how hard it is these days finding your kind of specialized work. You deserve the sleep as much as any early morning worker does. You deserve the wine, why not? I've been such a pill lately, maybe you deserve a woman in bed too."

"So come to bed with me."

"I didn't mean me."

"But I mean you. Let's make love. Get undressed. Have some wine yourself."

"I have to go to the restaurant in two hours."

"One glass won't kill you. Or no wine. Just come to bed. We haven't made love in a long time, probably because I've been so depressed at not finding work. So come on. It'll be nice. I'd like to."

"You don't feel too depressed and tired to make love?"

"No, I want to. I want us both to feel good and close together again."

"No, I don't think so. I don't feel like it."

"I'll make you feel like it."

"No, you couldn't. I appreciate the gesture, but I have to feel like it myself. Sorry. Have a good sleep. Get drunk even. Maybe that's what you need."

"You kidding?"

"No. Have a good time by yourself. I'll stay in the living room. I'll even sleep there for the next two days if you think that's the kind of absolutely peaceful rest you need to get up from your tiredness and everything totally refreshed. Sweet dreams," and she comes over to me and I stand and we kiss. I grab her behind with both hands. We continue to kiss.

"You're a faker," I say. "You want to make love. You just want to be coaxed. So all right, you're being coaxed. And as if I could sleep two whole nights without you beside me in bed."

"Maybe I do need to be coaxed, you goof-off. I really wasn't feeling too good with you before but now I'm feeling better. Yeah, I can spare an hour. It could be fun. Heck, I'm going to make it fun, because I need some fun too. You think slinging trays all night five nights a week is fun?"

"No."

"You're right." She starts taking off her clothes. "It isn't. It's tough. You know. You've seen me. It doesn't pay anything much either for all the hard work I put into it. And personal satisfaction from the job? Oh yeah, you bet. But I do it because we need money just as you'd do it if our situations were reversed. And things won't always be this tough for us, will they?"

"I can't say. I don't know. I can only say I hope not."

She's all undressed. I sit on the bed and she sits on my leg. "Maybe I should even call in sick today," she says.

"No, we need the money too much. They might fire you besides. Waitress jobs aren't easy to get either."

"Maybe my being fired will make you look harder for work."

"Don't throw out the old fish water—you know what my mother says. And I look hard enough. That's why I'm taking this rest today."

"Maybe they'll appreciate me more if I take a day off too. They'll say nobody waits on tables as fast as Lynn or is as honest."

"Are you that honest? Really?"

"Very honest. You know me. I never take a dime that isn't mine."

"I know. Maybe you're right. Maybe they'll think that. Maybe you should take off for one day. So what? Thirty dollars we'll lose, that's all.

Monday, though, I promise I'll look even harder for work than I've been doing, if that's possible."

"Okay, I'm taking the day off. Don't do anything without me," and she leaves the room.

I hear her on the phone in the next room. "My husband's not feeling too well. In fact he's feeling absolutely awful. I have to take him to the hospital, I think. Stomach pains, very severe, maybe only the flu, but I don't want to take any chances. He's all I have."

She comes back. "Maybe I should have some wine too, now that I'm not working."

"Go on. Get me another glass too. If there's only enough for one glass, you have it all."

"No, we'll share. Share everything today and tonight. Share our day off, share our bodies, share the bed. Share the wine, the food, the cleaning up. What else is there to share? Everything."

She leaves the room. I get in bed. She comes back with the wine jug and a glass. "Enough for more than two glasses of wine in it," she says. She pours some wine into my glass, empties the jug into hers. "So, I was wrong." She drinks. "No, we should've toasted first. Here's to us and better employment and a good time today, tonight and all weekend and Monday for you when you find a new great job."

"Here's to all of that and especially my getting a job," and we clink glasses. Then we kiss, drink and kiss. She sits on the bed. I touch her back, run my finger down her spine crack to the top of her buttocks.

"That feels cold but good," she says.

"Come on, get in."

"Don't mind if I do." She gets into bed. We start kissing and fondling. The phone rings.

"Let it," I say.

"I can never let a phone ring at any hour. It could be important. My mother and something wrong."

She jumps out of bed and runs to the phone. I hear her talking.

"What? . . . I already told you, his stomach. . . . What? . . . Oh please, what a story they're giving you. I bet if you checked you'd find the two of them in a movie together. . . . Yes, I understand the difference. They're sick themselves while with me it's only my husband.

Thanks a lot. . . . Yes, I think he can manage alone. I'll ask him. Hold on."

She comes into the room. "Tell him to drop dead," I say.

"If only I could. But until we find better work, this is what we have to put up with. I'll have to go in unless you can come up with a good excuse for me. Janine just called in sick and when he called Alberta to come in earlier, she said she was just about to call him that she had a flu and couldn't come in too."

"They're both lying."

"I know. But that's what I should've come down with when I phoned him about you. It isn't all bad though. Even if he can convince the day girl to stay, there'll still be only two of us and I can make a lot more than I usually do. In fact . . . no, you're supposed to be sick, but if only you could come in with me."

"Tell him I recovered."

"You mean it?"

"Either way he'll think we're lying, so what's the difference? Tell him a miraculous sudden recovery when I smelled the dollars I could make. He'll forget the lie and just be happy you got someone so fast to work there."

"You remember how to wait tables?"

We hear a long whistle from the phone.

"If I have trouble you'll help me, right?"

"Right. Oh, I love you." She runs back to the phone. I hear her talking on it. "You wouldn't believe it. I went back to the room where my husband was resting and he was up and said he had a miraculous sudden recuperation—a little of it, I'm convinced, when he thought of all the money he could be making tonight. What I'm saying is that he now feels great, maybe he was faking it before just to have me stay home, and wants to know if you could use him to replace Janine and Alberta tonight. He knows how—he waited on tables for years. . . . Great. See you at the regular time. . . . Earlier? How much earlier? . . . Oh damn. Oh well. It'll mean I'll make even a little more money. See you."

She comes into the room. "He needs me there now. You, he said, can come in when I usually do. At five sharp, okay?"

"Do they feed me too?"

"Sure."

"Good. We save that way too. Come on back to bed. Let's do it quickly."

"No time. Now, he said, he wants me there now."

She picks her pants off the floor and starts to put them on. I get out of bed and walk toward her with my arms straight out in front of me. "I don't know if that walk means you're coming over to drag me back to bed," she says. "But if it does, you better start thinking about something else."

"I was thinking of it."

"Then think of something else. And don't drink any more also. You have to be sober to wait on customers and it's better for your tips to have no alcohol on your breath."

"I wish life was easier," I say, getting back in bed.

"You mean you wish it would always go the way you want it to. That would be so boring."

"Not 'always.' Just 'almost.' "

"Even 'almost always' would be too boring." She finishes dressing, kisses me on the lips good-bye. "Come at least quarter to five so I can show you how the operation works."

She leaves. I set the alarm and go to sleep. The alarm rings at 4:30 and I shut it off and try to sleep some more. The hell with waiting on customers, making a quarter tip here, a dollar or two there. I'll get a good-paying job Monday—definitely some kind of job one day next week. I know she'll be angry if I don't show up, no matter how much in tips she makes tonight. But I'll explain to her later that I really did suddenly get a sharp stomach pain like an appendicitis attack, "unbelievable as this must sound to you," I'll say. "I tried calling the restaurant a couple of times but the line was busy. Then I couldn't even get to the phone the pain was so bad."

But she'll call around five when she sees I'm not there and if I don't answer the phone, she'll call at ten after five and so on and if I don't answer after those times, she'll think something's really the matter with me and maybe cab over here. If I do answer the phone when she calls . . .

no, the whole lie's too complicated to carry out and she can get fired be-sides. It's already ten to five and I shave and put on black pants and black shoes and a white shirt and stick a tie in my pocket and grab a cab outside and go to the restaurant.

"Where've you been?" she says when I walk in. "I just finished dial-ing you. The manager's rabid and was ready to fire me after tonight."

"That's what I was afraid of. I'll explain to you later but apologize to him now."

"Do that. Then come right back out here, and put on your tie."

I go in the kitchen and say to the manager "I'm sorry, Mr. Silo. I was taking a nap just to rest my stomach a little from before and overslept."

"Your stomach, huh? Look, just do a neat job and don't offend no customers or the cook and we'll forget you ever came so late and scared me half to death."

"Thanks."

Lynn shows me around. "If I see you falling behind I'll help you out. You see dirty dishes on my tables or someone wants water or bread, help me out with those too. Cooperate and it'll be a lot easier for us than it is for me with my regular coworkers. They're only out for themselves."

I do a good job, keep my station clean, don't break anything, remem-ber who gets what and when and help Lynn and she helps me and to-gether we make three times the tips she usually does in one evening.

"That's because we cooperated," she says when we're setting up the floor for the lunch shift. "If you really knew your way around here we would've made even more than that. I wish I was working with you every night. Our wages and tips were as good as the money we made when both of us were working at different jobs a year ago, and I'd get to see a lot more of you too. What do you say?"

"To become a waiter here?"

"Why not? I'll ask Silo. He'll probably go for it. The restaurant will save paying one more server and he thinks the other two are sloppy and lazy. We'll do it together for maybe a year and put away enough to take a vacation next summer and even live reasonably well for a change."

"But Alberta and Janine will be out of work."

"Stop it. They complain all day about being waitresses and both their husbands have good-paying jobs anyway. One's a cop, the other runs a laundromat. I forget whose is which, but one can work for the laundry and the other can afford to stay home and think about her complaints for a while."

"What about the union?"

"Silo slips the union man a twenty and it's made."

"Okay. Maybe it'll end my depression also. Maybe all I need is any kind of work—just some money of my own coming in. And it might be fun working with you, who knows?"

She goes over to Silo. I overhear her say "My husband and I would like to stay on as a team. We'll come in six nights a week just like I do now for five. You won't need Alberta and Janine and they're always being undependable. What do you say? You saw how good he was only his first night here. In a week he'll be so good he'll be able to handle the place alone if I'm ever sick one day, which I won't be, I promise. If he ever gets sick, which is also unlikely, you know I can handle the place alone for any amount of days."

"I like it. Those girls give me headaches. Let me make a call."

Lynn turns to me and smiles and puts up her fingers in a victory sign.

Silo phones someone, puts down the receiver. "I got the union fellow at home," he tells Lynn. "He says I've no grounds for bouncing the girls. That if I really want, it'll take weeks of my reporting they're filthy and unreliable for me to get them out."

"You can't give him a little bonus? Take my wages for a couple of days if that's what'll do it."

"He's not the type and I'm surprised you thought I was like that too."

Lynn comes over to me. "Well, I tried," she says. "Ready?" and we say good night to Silo and walk home.

Next day without any urging from Lynn I look for a waiting job and get one at the third restaurant I go to. It's not what I had in mind for a job a day ago but I've at least got one now. I feel good about it. I go home and tell Lynn. She says "So last night was a lot more for you than you thought, right? When do you start?"

"Tonight, same time as you."

She looks at her watch. "We've one hour then to have a glass of wine, jump into bed and make love. Quick," and she takes my hand and we go to the kitchen. I remember there's no wine, so we open a couple beers, clink the cans, toast to next summer's vacation and go into the bedroom and take off our clothes and get in bed. "Wait," she says when we start kissing.

"For what?"

"The phone."

"I didn't hear it ring."

"That's it. I don't want it to." She gets out of bed and leaves the room and I suppose takes the receiver off. By the time she comes back to bed I know she's taken the receiver off. I hear that off-the-hook beeping noise.

"You have good ideas," I say.

"I usually end up working extra hard because of them, but they usually are good ideas."

I shut off the night table light.

"No, keep it on," she says, leaning over me and turning the light back on. "We might doze off after and sleep right through the night and then we'll both get canned."

DARLING

"Darling?"

I go to her room, turn on the light, stand by her bed.

"Could you turn me over please?"

I turn her over on her back.

"And get my pills?"

I go to the kitchen, turn the sink tap on and wait for the water to run cold.

"And don't forget a glass of water."

The water runs cold. I bring the pills and glass of water to her bed.

"I hope the water's cold."

I hold the pills out on my palm. She points to her mouth, sticks out her tongue. I put a pill on her tongue, hold the glass to her lips while I hold up her head with my hand. She swallows. Then the second pill and water. She nods. They're both gone. She opens her mouth to show me: all gone.

"Could you turn me over, please?"

I turn her over on her stomach. I turn off the light.

"Thank you."

In a minute she's snoring. I leave the room. I get the mail which has been pushed through the mail slot of the front door. Around noon she'll call me again.

"Darling?"

I go to her room and raise the shade. She's still on her stomach. She can't turn over by herself though occasionally she still tries. She can't walk. She can't sit up or lie on her side for more than a few minutes without it causing her great pain. She never gets out of bed.

"Could you turn me over, please?"

I turn her over and give her today's mail. From the kitchen I get her soap, towel and basin of water so she can wash her mouth, face and hands.

"And you know what else."

I get the bedpan out from under the bed. While she's on it I cook all

151

of today's food. I bring her a tray of food, take the bedpan out from under her, empty the basin water into the bedpan and the bedpan into the toilet. I wash my hands. I help feed her what she can't feed herself, give her her afternoon pills and water, go to the front door and get the morning newspaper on the stairs of her building's stoop. Most of the time it's on the sidewalk in front of her house and only once a month is one of her two daily newspapers on her front door mat. I give her the newspaper. While she reads it I take away the opened mail, tray and basin with soap and towel, have my lunch, wash the tray, eating utensils and bedpan, hang up the towel, put the soap and basin into the cabinet under the kitchen sink, separate the bills from the correspondence and ads in the mail, put the ads into the kitchen garbage pail, the correspondence into a box in her living room desk and make out and have her sign the monthly checks for the grocer, druggist, doctor, utility and telephone companies and newspaper delivery service and place the last check under the doormat. I put away all the things I washed, do today's shopping and give the grocer and druggist their checks, return to the house and put away all the things I bought and get the afternoon paper at the front door. It's been carefully rolled up and bound with a rubberband and left on the doormat. I give her the paper. After she finishes it I put both newspapers on the pile of newspapers in the kitchen corner. Twice a month I tie the newspapers into three or four stacks and set them in front of the house with the week's garbage. I turn on her bedroom light and pull down the shade. I turn her over and turn off the light. She'll sleep on her stomach till around six.

"Darling?"

I go to her room and raise the shade. It's nearly dark.

"Could you please turn me over?"

I turn her over, heat her supper, turn on the light, give her her pills, water and supper, help feed her, take away the tray, pull down the shade, give her the bedpan, book she's been reading and needlework, have my supper in the kitchen, clean the tray, eating and cooking utensils, take away the bedpan and empty and clean it, put away everything I cleaned, put her book and needlework back on the dresser, turn her over and shut the light.

"I think tomorrow you'll have to bathe me and change the bed."

Of course tomorrow I will. She doesn't have to remind me. I sponge bathe her and change her bed every three days unless she's had an accident, and then it's every three days from the day of the accident. She hardly ever has an accident. The last was three months ago. Before that, six months ago. Before that, I don't know. I wasn't here. I never asked. She wouldn't tell me besides. I was living with my wife and child in another city at the time. Why'd I ever leave them? Because my wife threw me out. Said if I couldn't provide for them I couldn't live with them. Said they'd get more from Welfare by living without me than I ever gave them when they lived with me. I tried to earn enough to stay. For a while I had three jobs at once. But minor jobs, poor-paying jobs. In the morning I worked as a life model for a group of artists. In the afternoon as a sweater salesman in the men's section of a department store, but I got fired when I tried sticking some of the store's money into my pocket. On weekends I cleaned up the laboratories of a university's science building, but lost that job when they heard I'd been fired for stealing money from the department store. The artists kept me on despite knowing of my theft, but it wasn't enough wages for my family to live on. I went to several cities to find a well-paying full-time job, thinking that if I got one I'd get a nice apartment and have my family move in with me. But I never found any other work than part-time modeling for poor artists and cleaning up labs and such for universities and churches that didn't pay very much. Eventually I landed in this city. I answered a newspaper ad the day I arrived: *Young man to help elderly woman. Room and board plus adequate pay.* I called her with one of the last coins I had. She said come right over. There were three other applicants when I got here, two not that young so they were disqualified from the job. The third was much bigger and stronger than I, but too young and good-looking, she said. She told him he wouldn't stay the month: "You'll use my place as a flophouse till you catch the eye of a pretty counter girl, then leave me high and dry without even a day's notice." I was hired on the spot, given the room next to hers. Besides all the duties I mentioned, I do the laundry, see the doctor in and out of the house, and answer her call to me every night around ten.

"Darling?"

I go to her room, turn on the light, turn her over on her back.

"My evening pills, if you don't mind?"

I bring her the pills without water, I don't know why. Maybe so she'll have reason to fire me. I don't know if I want to be fired, but I think I do. This drudgery. I've had the job for seven months. This loneliness. If she fired me I might find a more interesting job, one that would pay me enough to afford an apartment and send for my wife and child. But I don't have the courage to quit, as not only wouldn't I be entitled to unemployment benefits but there's a good chance my next job would be even worse than this.

"You intentionally forgot the water."

I nod. She's right. Why try to fool her? I go to the kitchen, again let the water run cold. But no. I turn the warm water tap on, and bring her a glass. She drinks it with the first pill.

"It's warm. Now you know I like it cold. What's got into you tonight?"

I raise my shoulders, go to the window and raise the shade.

"You know I like the shade down when it's dark."

I lower the shade.

"The cold water, please?"

I go to the kitchen.

"You forgot the glass."

I return to her room, take the glass from her hand.

"Only half a glass of cold water. I already took the first pill with the warm."

I go to the window.

"Please don't raise the shade again."

I empty the glass onto the floor.

"Please clean that up."

I go to the utility closet for a mop, leave the glass on a shelf and return to her room.

"Please don't forget the cold water. I want to go to sleep."

I turn off the light.

"Not before I've had my pill."

I turn on the light, turn it off and on repeatedly.

"Please?"

I leave the light on.

"The cold water?"

I begin mopping the floor.

"First the cold water."

I get the glass from the utility closet, go to the kitchen, bring her a glass of cold water and spill it over her bed.

"You did that intentionally. Now you'll have to change my bed. Also my gown. And you still have to get me half a glass of cold water. And then finish mopping this floor. That's all you have to do. Besides turning me over and shutting off the light."

I turn her over.

"I didn't mean for you to turn me over right now."

I turn her over on her back.

"And for mercy's sake, don't shut off the light now."

I shut off the light.

"I said 'For mercy's sake, don't shut off the light now.' "

I turn on the light. I mop the floor. While I'm mopping she says "All right, finish mopping the floor. At least get that out of the way. And once that's done, let me repeat for the last time what you still have to do, though I don't want you to start doing them till I tell you to. First of all, get me half a glass of cold water. Second, get clean sheets and a clean nightgown and make the bed and change me and then turn me over, turn off the light and go to sleep yourself. No, you can do what you want in your own room after you've done all those things, but first get all those things done."

I finish mopping the floor. I go to the kitchen and bring her half a glass of cold water. She drinks the water down with the second pill.

"Good. Now the linens and gown. But don't forget to return the mop."

I wring the mop out above the utility sink, hang it up in the utility closet, get a broom from that closet and sweep up the kitchen. I continue sweeping into the hallway and then into her room. I sweep under her bed.

"Please don't sweep under my bed. You'll dirty the bedpan."

I sweep the side of her bed, the blanket over her bed, the sheet across her shoulders.

"Please get the clean bed linen and gown."

I return the broom to the utility closet, get a dustpan from the closet and with my hands and feet push onto it the piles of dirt I left in the two rooms and hallway I swept in, empty the dustpan into the kitchen garbage pail, put the dustpan back on its closet hook, get two clean sheets and pillowcases out of the linen closet and return with them to her room. I begin changing her bed with her in it. It's something she taught me how to do from her bed the first day I got here, and I've been able to do it without her instructions ever since. After rolling her from one side of the bed to the other to get the old sheet off and new sheet on, I tuck in the top sheet, change the pillowcases, lift her head, stick the two pillows underneath and gently lower her head to the pillows.

"Finally you do something right. Thank you. Now the blanket and my gown if you don't mind."

I raise the shade.

"Please lower the shade."

I go to the kitchen, fill a glass with warm water, go to her bedroom and empty the glass on her.

"Now you'll have to change the bed again. It's a good thing you didn't put on the blanket. Please get another clean set of linens. Though before you do, lower the shade."

I lower the shade. Then I raise and lower it repeatedly till she says "Will you please keep it lowered. Then get the linens, change the bed for the last time tonight, get my gown, help me change into it, turn me over, place the blanket on top, dump all the old linens into the washing machine, shut the light and get out of this room."

I go to the laundry room with the old linens, stick them into the washing machine, add a cup of detergent, go to the adjoining cubicle, turn on the hot and cold water spigots of the cubicle's utility sink which is attached by long rubber hoses to the washing machine, and return to the laundry room and start the machine.

"Darling?"

I go to my room and sit on the bed. On my dresser is an empty frame. Yesterday I removed the photograph of my wife and child from the frame and tore it up. Then I began putting the photograph back together and have half of it done now. It's like a picture puzzle which is getting easier and easier to solve. I have most of my son's face, none of my wife's, all of her knees, calves, ankles, both her socks and shoes, and all the grass they're sitting on. When I get the photo together again I'll cover it with cellophane tape and stick it back in the frame.

"Darling?"

I throw the frame against the wall. It splits in two, the glass shatters on the floor. Of course I'll never be able to get the glass together again, while the frame I can. I get a hammer and nails from the tool chest in the garage and start to fix the frame.

"Darling?"

I go to her room.

"I hope you're not planning to use that thing on me."

I forgot I was holding the hammer. I return it to my room, go to the kitchen, bring her a glass of water and place the water to her lips while I hold out the pills.

"I already took my pills, thank you."

I forgot that too. I return the pills and water to the kitchen, dry the glass and put it back into the cupboard, get the mop out of the utility closet and begin mopping her bedroom floor.

"You've already done that."

That's right, I have. I raise the shade.

She shakes her head.

I pull down the shade and turn off the light.

"Darling?"

I turn on the light and turn her over.

"Not yet, please."

I turn her over on her back, get fresh linen from the linen closet and begin changing her bed.

"That's fine. Very good. You know how to do this extremely well. I'm sure you'll be able to get a hospital orderly or nursing home job any time you want, just by the way you change a patient's bed."

I finish changing the bed and shut off the light.

"Not before I'm in a fresh gown, on my stomach and covered up."

I turn on the light, sit her up, slip off her gown, bring the gown, linen and mop to the laundry room, take the washed linen out of the washing machine and stick it into the dryer, put the gown, used linen and detergent into the washing machine, start both machines, return the mop to the utility closet and get a nightgown out of her dresser. As I'm pulling the nightgown over her I look at her chest. She has many brown blotches there, a new growth, long scars on her neck and back from her last operation when she had several growths and some muscle removed. She's still very ill. The doctor told her she'll never again be able to leave a bed. She never speaks directly of her illness or incapacity, though she's often mentioned how much she misses taking walks and just being well. I hug her. I want to hug her tighter, but fear it might hurt her and even cause injury. I cry on her shoulder and she pats my back.

"There, that's okay. This job can get you down sometimes—I know. And I'm not getting any better to look at or easier to handle. And what I say can occasionally get anyone down. You're very sensitive in many ways. It's not healthy for you to be in this kind of work, though I suppose it's better for the people you take care of. You're a little eccentric at times as we all probably are, but deep down you're very kind. Just try and deal with me and my situation the best way you can."

I kiss her shoulder and cheek, finish dressing her for sleep, lie her on her back, turn her over on her stomach, cover her up and tuck in the top sheet and raise the shade.

"Please lower the shade. Leave it up then. What harm will it be but a little morning light waking me up sooner than I planned. I'll simply pull the covers over my head and fall back to sleep that way."

I pull down the shade.

"Keep it down if you wish."

I raise the shade.

"It's fine that way too."

I turn off the light.

"Good night, darling."

I turn on the light and lower the shade.

"Then I'll sleep with the light on and shade down."

I raise the shade, lower it slowly, tear it down and kick it around and pick it up and smash it against the windowsill.

"If you're through, I'll again say good night."

I tear the shade into many pieces, toss them around the room, get the broom from the utility closet, sweep up the shade pieces and dump them into the garbage pail in the kitchen, sweep up the broken glass in my room, dump the glass into my wastebasket and empty the basket into the garbage pail, bring the broom back to the utility closet and return to my room with the basket.

I work on my photograph. I find my wife's head. I haven't found her neck yet, so I've no place to put the head. In the photograph my son sits on my wife's lap, his body concealing her belly and chest. I find her neck attached to her shoulders, place this piece and the head on the bottom half of the photograph I've put together so far. The photograph's now complete for my purpose. I get a roll of cellophane tape from the desk in the living room and tape the front of the semicomplete photograph.

"Darling?"

I go to her room, reach down for the shade string, reach up for the string, remember there is no shade, turn off the light, return to my room and tape the back of the photograph.

"Darling?"

I go to her room with the roll of tape and fasten several strips over her mouth.

"Dlung?"

I turn on the light and return to my room.

"Darling?"

I go to her room, turn off the light, stand above her bed and look down at the back of her head made visible by the streetlamp light.

"Turn me over, please?"

I turn over the bed.

"Ring the doctor, please?"

I call the doctor, sit by the front door till I hear his car pull up, open the door as he rings the bell. He sets down his bag, gives me his coat and hat, goes into her room with his bag, comes out without it.

"She's had an attack. And broken a bone in the fall. I'm afraid it looks very bad." He calls for an ambulance.

I put on his coat and hat and leave the house. I stand in front of her building. The air's cold. The sky seems empty of stars. Both curbs are packed with parked cars. The doctor's is the only car double-parked, its emergency lights flashing. An ambulance pulls into the street with its siren on and double-parks behind the doctor's car. The siren's turned off. The two ambulance men run around to the back, pull out a stretcher and go into the woman's house with it. They come out bearing the woman on the stretcher. The doctor, wearing one of the woman's fur coats, walks beside her holding her hand.

"Wait."

The bearers stop sliding the stretcher into the ambulance. The doctor says push it all the way in as they have to get to the hospital fast.

"Wait."

"Okay. Do as she says. Wait for a second, but no more."

The woman beckons me to her with her finger. A bearer braces up the back half of the stretcher which extends out of the ambulance's rear door. The other bearer lights up two cigarettes and sticks one between the first bearer's lips. The doctor rests the woman's hand on her chest, takes his hat off my head and brushes it off. The woman takes my hand in hers.

"Don't forget to turn off all the lights. And shut and lock all the windows. And make sure the oven and all the stove burners are off. And the furnace is switched off. And all the electrical plugs are pulled out of the walls. And all the faucets are turned off tight. Then leave the house and lock the door. But *leave* the house. Drop the keys through the mail slot. I'll have the doctor phone the newspaper delivery service and post office to temporarily suspend service. He also took my keys and left your week's wages and two weeks' severance pay on my dresser. You may take my valise if you feel it'll be of more use to you than your own. It has my initials on it so I suggest you blacken them out. If I survive all this and am discharged from the hospital, I'm going to place a notice in the newspaper for a man needed to help an elderly woman. I'll stress that he be middle-aged and reasonably educated and strong, and this time I'll insist on references I can verify. I don't think I'll be confined so long that by the time I'm discharged you'll be middle-aged, so you needn't apply for the job if you see the ad. Good-bye."

She lets go of my hand. The doctor puts a note under his car's windshield wiper, signals the bearers to slide the stretcher all the way into the ambulance and for me to give him back his coat. He hands me the fur coat, puts his own coat on, climbs in after her, sits next to her, puts on his hat and adjusts it and takes her wrist pulse. The bearers step on their cigarettes, climb in front, turn on the siren and the ambulance drives off. I watch its revolving roof light till it's just a blinking speck in the distance. Then it disappears. I look up. The sky still seems empty of stars.

I go into her house, hang up her coat, put on my jacket, take the money off the dresser and stick it into my pocket. She didn't include half of the two weeks per year vacation pay for the seven months I worked, but I'm lucky to get what I did. I remove the shade from my bedroom window and put it on hers. I lift up the bed, make it, pick the pieces of cellophane tape off the floor, pull down the shade, pull out the lamp and radio plugs, shut off the light and go to the kitchen, put the pieces of tape into the garbage pail, make three stacks out of the corner pile of newspapers, bind them with cord and cut the cord with the scissors I get out of the utility drawer, return the cord and scissors to the drawer, carry the pail and newspaper stacks outside and leave them in front of the house, go to the laundry room and take the first batch of linens out of the dryer and fold them up, take the nightgown and second batch of linens out of the washing machine and stick them into the dryer, turn the dryer on, put the folded linens back into the linen closet, turn off the hot and cold water spigots of the utility sink in the cubicle, pull out all the electrical plugs in the living room, my bedroom and kitchen, and make sure the faucets in the bathroom and kitchen are turned off tight.

I go to my room and try to piece together the top half of the photograph. The last piece I insert to make the top half complete shows a barn on a hill with part of a mountain behind it. I tape both sides of the top half, tape the two halves together to make the photograph complete, nail the frame together, put the photo into the frame, make my bed, dust the room with an undershirt, put the roll of tape back into the living room desk, get my valise out of my closet, take it outside and leave it on top of the newspaper stacks, get my toothbrush out of the bathroom holder and the woman's valise from the hallway closet, put my clothes, toothbrush, framed photograph, book and wallet inside the valise, zip it up, get paint, paintbrush and turpentine from the paint rack in the garage, shut the furnace off in the garage and lock the garage door from the inside, black out the woman's initials with the paint, moisten the undershirt with turpentine and clean the brush with the shirt, return the paint, brush and turpentine to the paint rack and hammer and unused nails to the garage tool chest, put the shirt into the furnace, take the gown and linens from the dryer and fold them up, pull out the electrical plugs of the washer and dryer, put the linens into the linen closet and gown into her dresser, shut and lock all the windows, turn off all the lights, leave the house with the valise, lock the front door and drop the keys through the mail slot.

I walk downstairs and away from the house. Halfway up the street I remember I didn't check to see if the oven and stove burners were off. I run back to the house with the valise, go around to the back and look through the kitchen window. Two burners I used to heat up her supper are still on. I put the valise down, find a large flat stone and wedge it between the window sash and sill and with all my might I try prying the window open. The window springs up and the pane breaks from the force of the window hitting the lintel. The wind knocks a napkin holder off the kitchen table as I'm pushing the glass chips off the sill. The holder lands on the floor. A paper napkin falls out, floats above the stove, lands on one of the lit burners, ignites, one part of it quickly disintegrating while the burning part flies higher and ignites a window curtain. By the time I climb through the window, a kitchen cabinet has caught fire. I spray water on it from the sink faucet, but now the wall is on fire. I leave the kitchen through the broken window, pick up the valise and am running to the fire alarm box on the street when I hear sirens and see fire trucks turn the corner and pull up in front and behind the doctor's car. A fireman pushes me aside so the hose won't be dragged over my feet. Another fireman breaks open the front door and goes into the house, comes out and yells "Nobody's home from what I can tell." I stand across the street with a crowd of people and watch the firemen try to put the fire out and the house burn to the ground. The firemen pull in their hoses and leave. The entire crowd but a next-door neighbor leaves. A policeman stands guard in front of the debris.

"Terrible," the neighbor says to me and goes into her house.

I pick up the valise and walk several blocks till I come to the avenue. The avenue leads to the boulevard that leads to the highway that takes one out of town. About two miles away the highway hooks up with the superhighway that goes across the entire country, one of its last exits being the city my wife and child live in, the one I left nearly a year ago.

Maybe my wife will take me back. I'll promise to work very hard, never steal from a store, try and get three jobs again if that's what it takes to keep us going, even four if I can. A car comes along. I stick out my thumb.

"Where to?"

But what for? I've most of my seven months' wages, so I can afford to take a plane. Why lose time on the road when I can be home tomorrow and already looking for a job? My savings aren't much but enough for us to live on for a couple of months if it takes that long to find work. If it takes longer, she'll throw me out. I know her well. I wouldn't blame her one bit. A man should provide for his wife and child, no matter how tough it is for him to get and hold a job. I smile my thanks to the driver, wave him on, cross the avenue and wait for a hitch or bus to the airport. But it's late and by daybreak no other cars have come.

THE FRAME

I go into an art gallery and framing shop. The door's unlocked. I'm surprised. Last time I got something framed here a woman let me in with a buzzer. And when I came back to pick up the framed work she let me in with a buzzer. A different woman sits behind a long table at the end of the room. "Yes," she says on the phone, nodding at me, "I tried to get it. . . . No, it was the wrong color but the right size. . . . Uh-huh. Uh-huh. Yes, but look it, a customer just walked in, so. . . . Uh-huh." I'm comparison-shopping. There's another art gallery and framing shop several blocks closer to my apartment. I came downtown to buy tofu at a natural foods store a few doors from this shop and to see about getting this—what would I call it?—framed. A photocopy. A friend of mine in Maine does photocopies as art. This one's of a heron's feather. She wrote on the matting "Feather of a Heron—to Jay Weiss." I can't get one of the standard picture frames at an odds and ends store for it, since the matting is a nonstandard size.

The woman says on the phone "It happened two weeks ago, I didn't plan it. It just happened." The look she gives me says "Please bear with me, I can't get off the phone." She's physically deformed. Her chest. She almost has no neck. It's sunk into her chest or her chest has risen above her neck. That's not accurate. She reminds me of my sister. She's about twenty years older than my sister was when she died fourteen years ago, but my sister—no. I was going to say my sister looked as old as this woman. She looked unhealthy since she was ten, then very sick, then at twenty-five, the last year of her life, deathly sick, but she never looked older than she was. The woman's deformed like my sister was. At least it seems so, in that sitting position, the way my sister would sit: top half of her body bunched up. Something. The bones of her chest way up, her back humped. With my sister it was something to do with the series of operations she had on her spinal cord and through her back and chest. I've an idea of what this woman's body will look like when she stands, if she can. My sister in her last years could stand, but only with the aid of crutches. The crutches were stretched out to the sides, like legs spreading to a split, when she just stood in place. When she walked, the crutches were thrown forward one at a time. And metal braces, not crutches. I knew the words then. I'll never forget the sounds. I still hear them occasionally in the school I teach at. The clink-clink of a disabled but not deformed young man using metal braces to walk down the hall past my open office door. Sometimes we look at each other through my door and nod or I say "How you doing?" or "Hi." "That's right," the woman says on the phone, "but it wouldn't have been like that if you'd made him sign first. . . . It's true, it's ridiculous to argue—I won't even go into how often I warned you. But really, Helene, I have to go. The customer. He's getting impatient."

"No I'm not."

She mouths to me *It's okay,* says on the phone "I'll call you back, good-bye," and hangs up. "Sorry. Can some people talk? Oh boy. That one—well anyway, what can I do for you?"

"I came in to see about a frame for this." I feel sad. I did want to comparison-shop. To see which frame store's price was the lowest for a frame of the same quality. I'm taking the matted photocopy out of my book bag. It's a snug fit. I'm doing it carefully. "It's not a drawing. I actually don't know what to call it, though I'm sure you do, but it is paper and matted and I don't want to scratch or dirty it when I take it out." She's sitting, watching me slowly inch the matting out. But if the price seems at all reasonable, even a little above reasonable, I'll pay it because the woman reminds me so much of my sister. Because she looks like Kathy—her body. Face too: slightly—how can I put it?—frozen on one side and disjointed. Because if Kathy were alive maybe she'd be working in a place like this and I'd come in, customer she never saw before, and I'd want to give her my business to keep her in business or just working at this job and making sales if the store's not hers, just as I do with this woman now. All that's pretty confused, but I'd want to do something like that. To keep her involved with people in a decent business or job. Because without this store her life must be fairly lonely and sad. That true? Kathy wasn't lonelier or sadder than most people when she could still get around. She knew people in the neighborhood. She went to block parties and meetings. People took her to movies and concerts and museums and a few times on weekend vacations at their country homes or resorts out of town. She converted to Christianity near the end of her life and was very active in the church a few blocks from where she lived with my parents, and for one year was in its choir. She had real friends. People liked her. She was nicknamed the mayor of the block. Dozens of people came to her funeral and then to pay their respects to my parents and me when we sat in mourning for several days. The matted photocopy is out. It has a sheet of white paper over it, taped to the back of the matting on top by the woman who made the photocopy. I pull back the paper. "I'd like the least expensive frame possible for it."

She looks at it. "Black?"

"Oh, yes, black, no other color. It'd be right for it, right?"

"It's what I'd choose. You don't mind a very thin frame? It would be the cheapest."

"Thin as any black frame you have. It couldn't take more."

"Let's see then." She gets up and turns around. She doesn't need braces or crutches to stand. She faces many quarter-sections of frame models hanging on the wall. Black, brown, natural, gold and silver trim, fretted, metal, plastic, wood. "I know it's here. A lady ordered two yesterday, much larger frames than yours. Two by three almost. Maps." She's fingering through several black frame models. Her back's like Kathy's. Crooked on one side, the left. I forget which side Kathy's was. Right, I think. Left. I can't picture it. She finds a thin black frame model. "That one's just fine," I say.

"Let me see it against your artwork," she says. She fits the model over a corner of the matting.

"Fine," I say. "Looks nice."

She looks at the back of the model. *1.50* it says. A foot? Square inch? Is that a dollar-fifty? She runs a pencil down the second column of a chart on the table, then two boxes across. All the boxes have numbers in them and the further down and further across, the larger the numbers are.

"Honestly, this one's fine," I say. "The matting's okay? Not dirty?"

"Just a second." She multiplies some numbers on a pad. I'm looking at her face. She's about thirty years older than Kathy was when she died. She wears large loop earrings. Gold. Hoops with a diameter of about two-and-a-half inches. Kathy wore large hoop earrings but never that large. Her ears also were pierced. Got it done in an earring store when she was past twenty. She wanted to get them pierced long before then. I remember her saying something like "You'd think with all the touch-and-go operations I've been through, a simple ear piercing wouldn't bother me, but it did. I was absolutely petrified." "Fourteen seventy-five," the woman says.

"With the glass?"

"You wanted it with glass, didn't you?"

"Sure. It's just it's so cheap. You see, last frame I bought here was smaller and made of brown wood. An embroidery, I think you'd call it, of three horses which used to hang above my bed when I was a boy and which— Well, when I was in New York a few months ago my mother showed it to me and asked what had happened to the glass and frame on it. She'd found it in my old drawer under some things of mine when all this time for years she thought I had it or it was lost."

The woman's writing up the bill. "That so? An embroidery of horses? Here?"

"An old kind, mounted on a wood board. I think she probably got it fifty years ago. I didn't want to tell her I'd taken the frame and hid the embroidery more than fifteen years ago when I wanted to frame something I'd bought for a woman I was seeing at the time. I did things like that then. You learn. Anyway, the frame I bought here cost sixteen dollars plus tax and was about two inches shorter on each side and the wood was just as thin. There's something I'm maybe not seeing, but I don't mind. The price seemed fair then, and this one seems even fairer. Not only compared to one another, but by New York prices. I haven't lived here that long, but these frames are the only things I've bought in Baltimore that seem cheaper than the same things in New York, except the newspapers."

She finishes adding up the bill. "I don't remember that other piece. Horses?"

"Three of them only from their necks up sticking their heads through two stable windows, but seen from inside the stable. And I know how you operate," I say, taking out my wallet.

"You do?"

"The other woman who took care of me asked for half the framing price as a deposit."

"You don't have to. Your name and address?"

"You send a card when it's ready, I know. Jay Weiss. Nineteen East Twenty-ninth. But you don't want a deposit?"

"If you want. I don't care."

"Five dollars do?"

"Fine."

I put a five-dollar bill on the table between us, she writes "$5 dep" on the bill, tears the bill off the metal holder it's on and gives me the duplicate.

"In a month or so, right?"

"Yes. Thank you."

"You're welcome, and thank you."

She smiles, I smile, and as I turn to leave a man comes into the store. We pass each other. "I came back to look at that poster again," he says. I turn around. The walls have drawings and prints on them but are mostly filled with framed and unframed posters. Victorian men on bicycles, 1930's movie posters, Picasso and Miró museum retrospectives and art shows. The man's wearing a new trenchcoat and cowboy boots. The woman walks around the table to a large black portfolio leaning against a wall. She walks with a limp. Kathy did also from the time she was ten till she had to use braces to walk when she was around twenty-two. She was bedridden the last half year of her life, first at home where my mother took care of her, the last two weeks in a hospital. I was at her bedside when she died. I held her hand when she died. We were alone. The door was shut. It was a private room. I shut the door because I wanted to say things to her without anyone seeing or hearing me. Like "Kathy, you'll get better. Kathy, I love you. Kathy, don't worry. It's rough going now but I swear you're getting well. Kathy, it's Jay. Is there anything you need or that you want to say?" She said nothing that last day. I was holding her hand when she died. I didn't hear a death rattle. Someone told me there's always one, but I didn't hear it. I held her hand. The right, the left. Mostly the right because that was the one nearest the side of the bed I was best able to sit on. The other had life-supporting equipment and monitoring machines. I was looking at her face. I'm so sad now I'm about to cry. I held her hand, was holding her hand, which had been holding my hand a little when it just let go—no, I was holding her hand and felt that it wasn't holding mine when before it was, so I looked at it, squeezed it to feel if it would squeeze back. It didn't. I didn't let go of her hand. Her eyes were still half-closed as they'd been for most of the day. I looked at them. There didn't seem to be any movement in them when there was before. A dull movement before but movement. A blink every now and then when there wasn't any now. I had a feeling she had died. I put her hand by her side. I went out of the room, looked up and down the hall for a nurse, ran back into the room and got up close to her face. It was the same. Eyes half-closed. Tubes in her nose, but no sign of breathing. I went into the hall. A patient was walking for exercise. I'd seen him doing that many times before. I said "Please walk to the nurses' station and get the nurse." He said "It'll take me twenty minutes the way I go." "Stay here then and don't let anyone inside but a doctor or nurse." "I don't know if I can stay in any one place for very long." "Please," I said, "my sister. Don't be alarmed but I think she just died." "I'm so sorry," he said. "Of course I'll stay." I ran down the hall to the nurses' station.

"Is there anything wrong, sir—Mr. Weiss?" the woman says.

I look at her. The man, kneeling beside the opened portfolio on the floor, looks up at me.

"No, I was just thinking. Of my—why, don't I look all right?"

"The light isn't what it should be for this kind of store, but you look as if you suddenly lost all your color."

"No, I'll be okay."

The man's still looking at me. Then he looks at the woman and pulls a poster out of the portfolio and stands.

"Thank you," I say.

"You're perfectly welcome," she says. She holds up the other end of the poster and looks at it with him. I leave the store. Just then the elevator door opened and my mother walked out of it and started down the hall.

Design by David Bullen
Typeset in Mergenthaler Plantin Light
by Wilsted & Taylor
Printed by Maple-Vail
on acid-free paper